Honeymoon & Hemlock

Marriage & Mysteries

Abbey North

Published by Publishers' Portal, 2022.

This is a work of fiction. Similarities to real people, places, or events are entirely coincidental.

HONEYMOON & HEMLOCK

First edition. June 17, 2022.

Copyright © 2022 Abbey North.

ISBN: 979-8215045510

Written by Abbey North.

Blurb

Lizzy and Darcy are on their honeymoon in Bath when her mother and Kitty show up to surprise them. They have hardly recovered from that shock before they find a dead body in the women's changing room. The waters at Bath might heal, but they can't solve the mystery of who killed Lady Longe, or why they desired the cantankerous old woman's death. Lizzy and Fitzwilliam are the only ones interested enough to investigate the murder by hemlock and find answers. They have a knack for the endeavor, but Lizzy worries Fitzwilliam will lose patience with her undertaking, since it happens to be their honeymoon.

This is a spinoff from Abbey's popular "Crime & Courtship" series, which introduced mysteries to their romance. They are now married, but the mysteries continue, as does the evolution of their relationship.

While Abbey sometimes writes sensual JAFF, this is strictly SWEET.

Chapter One

Upon arriving at the hotel, Lizzy hadn't spared much thought or attention for looking at the interior, the decorations, or the details. She'd been more intent on reaching the suite she and Fitzwilliam had booked for the week in Bath, and that was where they had spent the first three days of their honeymoon trip.

Now, on the fourth day, they had decided to venture forth from their suite and enter the dining room in time for lunch. She couldn't help admiring the marble details along with the pretty silk wallpaper she lightly glided her fingers against as they crossed the room ahead of the maître d', who led them to a table in the open courtyard. It was a fine summer day, and not yet too hot to be sitting outside, especially since the restaurant had an awning.

"This is so lovely." She smiled across at her husband as she took his hand. "I am glad we decided to leave the room."

He grinned. "I am pleased you changed your mind. You seemed determined to stay there the entire week." There was a knowing gleam in his eyes.

Lizzy's cheeks flushed as she looked away, feeling a little shy despite days of shared intimacy with her new husband. It was so much more than she had expected, and when he'd suggested they leave the room this morning, she had been resistant to start with. Only his gentle persuasion and perseverance had gained her cooperation, and though she didn't regret it, she couldn't help looking forward to when they returned to the room later.

"All this fuss about food in the middle of the day," said a sharp tone from behind them, loud enough for the two of them to hear.

Reflexively, Lizzy turned to look over her shoulder, seeing an older woman with two younger women seated nearby.

"Aunt de Guille, it is the newest thing. We are told luncheon will become a regular part of everyone's life."

The older woman's scowl deepened. "Stuff and nonsense. A hearty breakfast, afternoon tea, and a good dinner are all you need. Perhaps a spot of supper every now and then if one is out late."

"I do not see the harm," said the woman who had called the older woman aunt. "In fact, I am feeling quite peckish and relieved I do not have to wait another two or three hours for high tea."

"My stomach is bothering me too much for this. Besides, eating is not why we are here, Estella," said the old woman.

"Lady Longe, we have not forgotten why we have come to Bath," said the other young woman in a soothing tone. "We are all hopeful it will make you feel better."

"It is terrible luck to be arriving just a few days before the shameful regent. I do hope I have sufficiently recovered to leave before his arrival." The old woman shook her head, her disapproval obvious.

Lizzy could hardly fault her, for she disapproved strongly of the Prince Regent as well. He was an adulterer, a liar, and a spendthrift. He was an inept father and husband, and she feared when their beloved King George III passed, he would make a mess of the country. She was glad their honeymoon trip was due to end before the Prince Regent's arrival.

"Have you had oysters before, Lizzy?" asked Fitzwilliam.

She looked away from the drama at the table behind her, determined to focus on her husband. "I have not. We do not often have them in Meryton, and Uncle Gardiner dislikes them, so I have not had a chance to try them even while in London."

His eyes gleamed with interest. "Might I suggest them? They have certain properties that I am certain you will enjoy, assuming the rumors are true." As he spoke, he stroked his finger down her wrist on the inside on her glove, making her shiver.

Lizzy was overcome with need for her husband, and she wished she had insisted on remaining in the room. "I propose we might try them, but I would rather order them for room service."

He frowned for a moment, but then he chuckled indulgently. "As you wish, my love." He stood up, holding out an arm as she laid her palm on his forearm. They nodded to the maître d' but made no explanation as they crossed the restaurant again, walked up the grand staircase, along with another two flights, and reached the room moments later.

IT WAS THE NEXT NIGHT before she felt ready to leave the suite again. It was her suggestion this time that they go down for dinner, but Fitzwilliam had made no argument, and he waited for her as she exited the bedroom, nodding her thanks to the lady's maid provided by the hotel before walking over to join him.

He offered his arm, and she accepted it before they walked downstairs together at a sedate pace. Once again, she was overwhelmed by the beauty of the hotel, which favored classical Greek architecture and decorations, though the style was only recently finding favor among Britons.

Once upon a time, she would've been easily flustered at the sight of the naked replica of David that dominated the lobby, but after having seen it compared to the real thing, it hardly seemed worth noticing now. Most certainly, poor David could not compare to her darling Fitzwilliam.

They reached the restaurant moments later, and it was the same maître d' who'd taken them to a table yesterday. If he recognized them, he gave no special recognition as he escorted them to a table, this time inside the restaurant. Lizzy accepted the menu offered a second later, spending a few minutes debating what she wanted to try that evening.

They had just placed their orders when there was a shrill cry from across the room. Lizzy jerked, as did Fitzwilliam, and the two of them turned to the source, with her expecting danger to follow. Instead, it was the same old woman as yesterday, though she looked far worse today. Her hair was scraggly and bedraggled around her face, and her clothes were disheveled. Her buttons were improperly buttoned, revealing her stays and shift beneath, and she appeared confused.

"Napoleon will kill us all," she shouted with conviction. "He arrives this night across the Channel."

There was a murmur of unease among the people at the restaurant, and Lizzy's stomach clenched as well. She turned to look at Fitzwilliam, who seemed as puzzled as her. "Do you think there is any truth to her words?"

Before Fitzwilliam could answer, the old woman said, "Cast not your pearls before swine. Thieves run amok, and Satan is in the garden with Eve. Time is drawing nigh."

The words were a series of rambling incoherence, and Lizzy wasn't the only person to reach that conclusion. The uneasy murmuring in the dining room changed, becoming one that was a little sharper, with a hint of mocking among most people.

"Perhaps we should help her," said Fitzwilliam as he started to get to his feet.

Lizzy was agreeable to the idea, and she stood up to join him, but before they could, the general manager of the hotel, whom they had met upon checking in, entered the dining room, and the two younger women who had been with the older woman yesterday were right on his heels. The three of them seemed to have it in hand, and though they couldn't subdue the woman, they managed to convince Lady Longe to leave with some persuasion on their parts, and what also looked like some sheer physical strength.

After a moment, she sat down again, not waiting for Fitzwilliam to hold her chair or assist her with it. He sat down after she had, and they both shared a long look. "That was certainly unsettling," said Lizzy.

"Indeed. I have seen older people diminished like that before, and it never fails to subdue me."

She nodded, recalling one such man who lived in Meryton. From what she knew of him, he had been perfectly normal until the last few years, when he started to lose his memory along with all awareness of his surroundings. She'd heard rumors that his daughter had to keep him locked in the house, or he would be roaming the village with no idea who he was or what he was doing. "It does seem a rather sharp decline quickly though."

Fitzwilliam waited to answer her because their server arrived, and they placed their orders, both opting for the specials of the evening. When the young man had taken their menus and darted away, he nodded. "I concur, but perhaps something has triggered an episode. Maybe she is more controlled at times unless other circumstances arise."

"Like someone who has fits. It only happens periodically?" She immediately recalled the boy who'd lived with the St. Croixes for a while, also a refugee from France. He'd been perfectly fine, except for fits that would seize him. He would fall to the floor spasming, and that could happen several times in a day. She grimaced as she recalled the poor young man had met an unfortunate end when one of his seizures had caused a him to strike his head and sustain an injury from which he had been unable to recover.

"We must not think about it too much, for we do not wish to ruin our honeymoon." As he spoke, a man approached wearing a starched red jacket, white breeches, and a sharply structured cravat tied in the Collier de Cheval style.

He bowed to both of them. "Good evening. I am the sommelier, and I am here to offer you suggestions on wine pairings."

Lizzy frowned. "I have not heard of such a thing." Admittedly, her dining experiences were relatively restricted, consisting of home, other families in Meryton, occasional parties in London, and a few tearooms.

"It is quite the standard in France," said the young man with a sniff that tried to diminish Lizzy for not knowing that.

Her lips twitched with amusement, but she managed not to laugh. She had no idea if his claim was credible, since the continent was closed for easy travel due to Napoleon's war, but it sounded convincing when delivered in such a fashion.

"We shall forgo the wine in favor ofchampagne, young man," said Fitzwilliam, though he could be only five or six years older than the man waiting on them. "We are here for our honeymoon."

"Excellent. I shall bring you a bottle of Dom Perignon."

"That sounds wonderful," said Fitzwilliam.

As the sommelier turned away, Lizzy whispered, "It also sounds expensive."

Her husband lifted a shoulder in a careless fashion. "We do not intend to indulge every night, do we? I see no harm in an occasional splurge."

Lizzy nodded her agreement, and the rest of the meal passed in pleasant conversation. The incident with Lady Longe had practically fled her mind by the time they left the dining room, and she only recalled the situation because when she looked down, she saw one of the lady's slippers.

She bent to pick it up, taking it with her to the front desk as Fitzwilliam trailed behind her. She handed it into the clerk, explained its origin, and then took Fitzwilliam's arm and walked with him up the stairs. The dinner had been wonderful, but she was ready to return to their suite, though she didn't feel the least bit tired just yet.

Chapter Two

Fitzwilliam found marriage most agreeable, and to his amazement, he and Lizzy had yet to exchange any sort of argumentative words. He had expected there to be at least a few disagreements, or more than a passing trade of banter, but they were both content, and he was hopeful for a blissful remainder of their honeymoon.

They were booked at the hotel for ten days, and with six days remaining ahead of them, he hoped they might actually leave the room for more than an hour or two. Of course, there was certainly no reason to complain about staying in either, and he smiled as he recalled how pleasant it was to wake with his wife in his arms.

He was still smiling when he caught a glimpse of an outrageous ostrich feathered-hat in the crowd. Something about it was familiar, and his eyes narrowed as he looked away from his breakfast plate to focus.

The hat was coming toward him, and as people moved out of the way, naturally shuffling as they headed to their tables, he got a good glimpse of the face under the hat. For a moment, he convinced himself he was simply hallucinating, but after blinking twice and even rubbing his eyes, the hallucination failed to dissipate, confirming it was all too real.

"My darlings," called Fanny Bennet much too loudly, while she was still too far away from their table to make a polite greeting.

Lizzy stiffened, as did Fitzwilliam, and he felt like there was a juggernaut inevitably and inexorably looming over him, about to crush them in its path. The juggernaut was in the accompaniment of one Kitty

Bennet, and the two women reached the table, not bothering to wait for an invitation before sitting down.

"Mama, what are you doing here? We are on our honeymoon," said Lizzy in a repressive fashion. Her color was high, and she was clearly displeased.

Either her mother didn't notice or didn't care, because she waved a hand. "It as not as though we are staying in the same room with you, *Mrs. Darcy*," her mother said in a firm voice, though she giggled afterward. "We are simply here to take in the waters, and we thought it would be a lark to arrive at the same time as you."

"Are you surprised, Lizzy?"asked Kitty, who appeared completely oblivious.

"I could not be more surprised if I woke stuffed in a trunk, Kitty," said Lizzy with some starch in her tone. "I cannot believe you thought this was a good idea, Mama."

"Mr. Darcy, do tell my daughter she is overreacting."

Fitzwilliam felt like he was on the spot for the moment, with his mother-in-law staring at him in a confident fashion, clearly secure in her belief he would support her, while his wife was glaring at her own mother and growing tenser by the second. With a sigh, he reached out and took Lizzy's hand in a soothing fashion. "I am certain we shall manage."

Lizzy frowned at him, and she looked like she wanted to argue for a moment, but she must have realized the futility of the effort, because her shoulders slumped a second later, and she sighed heavily. "Yes, I fear we must."

"Perhaps you could speak to that foul man, Mr. Trentworth," said Fanny to him, her displeasure obvious. "He has placed us in a tiny room at the back of the hotel, claiming that because we did not have reservations, we have to accept what is available."

"I shall look into it," said Fitzwilliam as diplomatically as possible. He might ask if there was another room available for the women, but he did not want to push the issue too hard, because there was an adjoining room in their suite that he had no intention of offering to the Bennet women. That would be going too far indeed. It was bad enough to share his honeymoon with his mother-in-law and youngest sister-in-law, though there was no protesting now, for they were consigned to such a fate.

"What do you have planned for this morning?" asked Kitty. "I should very much like to enjoy the shops."

"As I have told you, we shall do just that," said Fanny, huffing a sigh at her daughter that suggested the topic had been introduced more frequently than she would desire.

"We did not have firm plans, but I believe I would like to take in the waters," said Lizzy, sounding like she was speaking through gritted teeth. "I suddenly feel the need for a tonic to calm my nerves."

"Your nerves?" Fanny waved a hand dismissively. "You have no idea the toll this travel has taken on my nerves, Lizzy. It began with the coach driver, who seemed to have a knack for hitting every rut in the road. I do not believe..."

Fitzwilliam pasted on what he hoped was an interested expression and nodded periodically, but he managed to filter out most of Fanny's complaints. He was still reeling from her audacity to show up at the same place and time where they were having their honeymoon.

Though he'd accepted Fanny Bennet had little regard for etiquette and manners, and she was certainly never one who was going to behave herself in the expected fashion, this was beyond the pale even for her. Counseling himself to find patience, he reminded himself she was a small price to pay to ensure Lizzy was at his side, and before they'd finished breakfast, he was finding more amusement than annoyance in the sudden arrival of his in-laws.

"You are going shopping?" asked Fitzwilliam as the meal wound down sometime later.

"Eventually," said Fanny, "But I believe I should like to take in the waters as well. They can only soothe my nerves, so we shall join you for that."

Lizzy looked close to apoplexy, and she opened her mouth, clearly intent on telling her mother she wasn't welcome, but Fitzwilliam reached out and touched her hand, squeezing lightly. "I do not see why that will be an issue, for the men and women bathe separately here anyway. You shall have someone to keep you company, Lizzy," he said in a soft tone as he looked at his wife.

She was still glaring at her mother, but after a moment, she nodded stiffly. "How wonderful," she said with a lack of conviction.

"Since we are all headed the same direction, I shall it accompany you ladies to the changing rooms." He stood up, moving first to assist Lizzy from her chair before walking around the table to do the same for Fanny and Kitty. Kitty giggled in a self-conscious fashion, and he realized abruptly that Lydia was missing. "I say, I am surprised to see you without Miss Lydia, Mrs. Bennet."

"She has gone to Brighton with the militia when they decamped Meryton. Her dear friend, Harriet Forster, who is married to Colonel Forrester—as I am certain you remember, Lizzy—" She looked at Lizzy, who nodded her confirmation. "She has gone to stay with her for a time."

"I do hope it is safe," said Lizzy, looking fretful. "There are a great many soldiers which might tempt her to do something foolish."

"Do not be so hard on your sister," said Fanny. "She is so vivacious that she can hardly help being friendly with the officers. It is their fault if they read more into her behavior than she intends."

Fitzwilliam thought about opening his mouth to warn Mrs. Bennet that fully grown men might not be trusted to control their responses, but he changed his mind. After all, she did have a point. It was incumbent upon the men to control their baser impulses and realize Lydia was just a flighty young girl finding her way in the world. It could still be dangerous though, because not every man could be trusted to have that level of control and awareness.

"I do hope she will be cautious," he said instead. It was a compromise between the lecture Lizzy clearly wanted to deliver and the complete carelessness with which Fanny seemed to regard the entire matter.

"It was dreadfully unfair," said Kitty, her lower lip protruding. "Mrs. Forster did not invite me to accompany them."

"You are not overly friendly with Mrs. Forster, are you?" asked Lizzy in a questioning tone.

Kitty scowled as she shook her head. "She has not liked me since we wore the same hat to Aunt Philips, and I pointed out I wore it better."

Fitzwilliam's lips twitched, and it seemed like a poor reason to dislike someone, but he imagined it was quite serious to young women.

As they left the dining room, they walked down the hall and followed a small crowd heading in the direction of the bathing rooms. When they reached the changing rooms, he paused at the door to the women's changing room.

There appeared to be no one else entering just yet, but a glance at the hours posted on the wall revealed everything should be open, though it might be too early for some to partake. He nodded his head at them, taking Lizzy's hand for a long moment. "I shall see you inside the room, and then we will be together again afterward."

He wished they had a separate area where married people could bathe together, but this hotel was frightfully strict about such things, and the better-known hotel in the area had been fully booked when he made inquiries about reserving a room for their honeymoon, since his inquiries had been on short notice. They likely segregated as well though. It would be scandalous to allow the unmarried of either gender to mix in such an activity.

He turned and walked away, but he didn't make it far before he heard a bloodcurdling scream that came from Kitty. Without regard for decorum, he turned and rushed back to the women's dressing room, dashing through the door. "Lizzy? Are you all right?" As he asked, he drew to a halt at the sight before him.

Lady Longe was cold on the floor, her back arched in a strange fashion, and her eyes were wide open. She seemed to have a scream tapped on her lips, but it had not had a chance to emerge before she met her end. He could not be certain how long she'd been there, but the woman was most assuredly dead.

Chapter Three

Lizzy stared in shock at late at Lady Longe's body, wondering how the woman had managed to come to this end, with no one noticing until now. It was still quite early in the day, so she assumed the woman's niece had slept in, but shouldn't her companion have noticed she'd gone missing? Surely, her abigail would have as well.

Lizzy wondered if there was already a discreet search underway in the hotel, but she was distracted by the sound of a shout of outrage when an older woman entered the room, drawing back at the sight of Fitzwilliam. "I say, sir, what sort of shocking behavior is this? This is the ladies' changing room."

Before Fitzwilliam could speak up to defend himself, Lizzy stepped forward. "Madam, I am certain you do not wish to be here right now."

She was a large woman, and she drew herself up fully, clearly trying to intimidate Lizzy. "I assure you, I do. I came to Bath to take in the waters, and I shall do so. This hooligan must depart immediately."

"I am not a hooligan, I assure you, madam," said Fitzwilliam in a cold tone.

"There is a dead body here," said Lizzy. If the woman hadn't been so unpleasant, she might've tried to temper her words more moderately.

The older woman paled and swayed for a moment before taking a step back and spinning on her heel. She rushed from the room within seconds, and Lizzy realized Kitty was breathing harshly, and her mother was wailing. She turned to them, gentle but firm when she said, "You will leave now. Go straight to your room and rest until we have dealt with this. We will come find you."

Unsurprisingly, Kitty was the first to recover, at least enough to guide their mother from the dressing rooms. Lizzy followed them, with Fitzwilliam behind her. She stood in front of the door, saying, "I shall ensure no one else enters. Perhaps you should fetch the manager, dearest?"

Fitzwilliam nodded immediately, pausing only to press a kiss to her cheek and squeeze her shoulder in a reassuring fashion before he turned and walked away quickly.

Lizzy paced in front of the door for the next few minutes, turning away three different guests. Two of them accepted the explanation that the room was closed temporarily, but the third insisted on a full explanation. Consequently, the young woman left considerably paler than when she had arrived.

Lizzy issued a sigh of relief when she saw Fitzwilliam approaching in the accompaniment of one she recognized as the manager, Mr. Horace Trentworth, who was a paunchy, middle-aged man with a balding head, though his suit was fastidiously bespoke, and he clearly cared about appearances.

The man behind him was a few years younger, and he was in much trimmer shape, with an air of competence Lizzy found encouraging. She had no idea what his role was, but having him there seemed to make the situation better.

"Step aside, young lady," said Mr. Trentworth with a sniff, nose angled into the air.

Lizzy moved aside, but she followed Fitzwilliam when he trailed behind the manager and the other man. "Who is he?" she asked softly of Fitzwilliam when they stood back a few feet from the body is the man move forward, indicating the man with the manager. Mr. Trentworth had taken a handkerchief and now pressed it against his face, blocking his nose. Lizzy realized there was certainly an unpleasant scent in the room, though she didn't know if it was from decomposition or something else.

"He is the surgeon here at the hotel. His name is Hillgate."

She nodded her satisfaction is the man knelt on the floor of the changing room, spending several long moments examining the body. He looked up once at Mr. Trentworth and her husband to say, "Will you offer me some assistance, Mr. Darcy? I need to change her position slightly to check something."

Mr. Trentworth sounded outraged when he said, "You cannot ask that of a guest."

The surgeon looked at him for a long moment, his expression inscrutable. "I suppose you wish to help me then, Mr. Trentworth?"

Muttering something, the manager stepped back, and Fitzwilliam stepped forward. Lizzy followed, getting a little closer, though the body appeared the same as it had before even when she was nearer.

The man was helping Fitzwilliam turn her slightly, and he nodded. "Vomitus and this bluing at her lips and fingertips...peripheral cyanosis, which indicates her respiratory system was failing." He leaned closer and sniffed lightly before wrinkling his nose. "I believe this woman has died from hemlock."

"A suicide at our hotel?" Mr. Trentworth was grasping his chest. "Such scandal, and the Prince Regent is coming to stay just next week. Oh, this must be kept quiet."

"I do not believe it was suicide," said Mr. Hillgate in a firm tone.

Mr. Trentworth paused. "Why ever not?"

"Someone who is suicidal will likely ingest a large dose of hemlock and die within hours. No doubt, she would have chosen her room to do so. However, if one is poisoned over a series of days or weeks with ever-increasing doses of hemlock, they tend to become more and more confused, have difficulty breathing, experience hallucinations, and have less idea of who they are. Is this not the woman who caused the disturbance last night in the dining room?"

It appeared to cost Mr. Trentworth a great deal, but he managed to step forward and look down, quickly nodding before averting his gaze. "It is."

"She was likely already acting under a fatal dose at that point, though she perhaps had at least one more dose in the intervening hours. Rigor mortis has not noticeably set in, so she has been dead less than four hours, I feel confident in saying, but I cannot narrow the window of time closer than that for the moment."

"We must fetch the constable," said Fitzwilliam.

Mr. Trentworth drew himself to his full height, glaring at her husband. "We shall do no such thing, Mr. Darcy. The woman had a heart attack. That is the end of it."

"She did not—" started the surgeon.

Trentworth held up his hand. "She did. It is obvious, and you would see that if you did not wish to make a name for yourself. No doubt, you are hoping to impress the Prince Regent when he arrives next week, having heard he is displeased with his current physician. I will not have your ambitions tainting this hotel."

"This is a possible murder investigation," said Fitzwilliam. "The right thing to do is to send for the constable, or perhaps even a Runner. Do you have any Runners in Bath?"

"I do not know, for we do not have scandal here. There is no reason to summon any sort of authority. The surgeon will pronounce her dead by heart attack, and we shall send for the undertaker. In the interim, store her somewhere inconspicuous, Mr. Hillgate." The manager glared at him. "I do not have to tell you what will happen if you do not follow my orders. I shall remind you, nonetheless. Even surgeons without references will have a difficult time finding a new position. Do you not agree, Mr. Hillgate?"

The surgeon was clearly annoyed, and he seemed perhaps even enraged, but he clenched his teeth and nodded once. "I shall ensure the body is stored properly until Wilkinson comes for it, Mr. Trentworth."

Mr. Trentworth glared at Fitzwilliam before sending a brief glance in Lizzy's direction. He looked appalled. "This is no place for your wife, sir."

Lizzy stiffened her shoulders. "You are greatly mistaken about that, Mr. Trentworth, just as you appear to be about the cause of death. If the surgeon believes she was murdered, I believe the surgeon."

"It does not matter what you believe, madam. It is my hotel, and my word will be accepted and followed to the letter. If you wish to disagree, I am certain you can find accommodations elsewhere." With those tart words, he turned and disappeared.

Lizzy exchanged a glance with Fitzwilliam. "He would rather risk losing a powerful patron like you than have this investigated as a murder. I wonder if he is hiding something?"

"Just incompetence," said Mr. Hillgate with confidence. "Mr. Trentworth is merely the manager here, and he knows the owners have been displeased with him for the last half-year. I suspect he understands that if this is handled indelicately, he will likely be replaced. He is many things, but I do not think he is a murderer."

Lizzy nodded, though she decided to reserve judgment about that until they had a chance to investigate. Thinking of that had her looking at Fitzwilliam, and he appeared resigned, as though he had read her mind.

She beamed at him, pleased that he had so quickly grasped her intention to investigate the matter. How could they not, when they had literally stumbled across the murder, and it was obvious Mr. Trentworth would do everything in his power to bury it and prevent a full investigation? The woman had appeared cantankerous, but she deserved a full inquest into her death.

Chapter Four

Fitzwilliam was unsurprised when Lizzy wanted to trail behind Mr. Hillgate, who had purloined two of the footmen from the kitchen to carry the blanket-shouted body through the hotel. They went through a series of staff corridors, which required only the minimalist amount of transport of the body where guests might see it.

They ran into a small handful, and Fitzwilliam was certain rumors would circulate throughout the hotel by the evening that someone had died there, but no one had gotten a good look at the body, save himself, Lizzy, and her mother and sister. They were hardly likely to have paid much attention, since they'd both been so shocked by this sight.

Truthfully, he had been as well, for no one expected to find a dead body, though perhaps he shouldn't have been terribly surprised with the events they had gone through during their courtship. It seemed oddly fitting that there was yet another mystery that presented itself on their honeymoon.

For his part, Fitzwilliam would be happy for that streak to break, though he couldn't deny there was a new sparkle in Lizzy's eyes, and her cheeks were flushed. She was invigorated by the possibility of investigation, though he knew it was nothing so sordid as joy in having one. She was motivated to help find the answer to whomever had done away with the older woman carried between the two young men.

They reached a room in the basement several minutes later, and the surgeon nodded to a table. "You can place her there. Hold on though." He took time to remove two wooden boxes of produce and set them on the floor before they laid the woman out. He nodded at the young men.

"You can go now, lads. Thank you for your assistance, and I do not need to warn you to be discreet. Mr. Trentworth is likely to be more zealous than usual with anyone who talks about this. I have no doubt he would be content to sweep the entire matter into nonexistence. I would not wish either of you to lose your positions over this."

"Yes, sir," said the younger one with a nod.

"We shall be discreet, Mr. Hillgate." The slightly older one of the two boys nodded and departed quickly as well.

"How did you reach the conclusion it was hemlock, Mr. Hillgate?" asked Lizzy as she stepped forward. She sounded calm and confident.

The surgeon winced for just a moment, and he glanced at Fitzwilliam, who was standing slightly behind Lizzy. He nodded his head, giving his permission for the man to answer, though he felt ridiculous having to do so. Anyone who knew Lizzy knew she could handle the reality of the situation.

"There are a few clues that made me conclude it, Mrs...." He flushed. "I apologize, but I do not remember your name."

"Elizabeth Darcy," said Lizzy.

Fitzwilliam got a tingle at the words, still enjoying hearing Lizzy say his name linked to hers. It made it somehow more and less real each time she confirmed she was now his wife.

"Mrs. Darcy, I based it on the account of her behavior last night, the fact that I saw her upon her arrival when she complained of abdominal issues, and mainly because of the vomit and her dilated eyes. Cyanosis was also a clue, though it is not as common as others." He tilted her head back slightly after unwrapping the blanket, and Lizzy bent closer.

Darcy gave a cursory look, but he didn't care to get too close. He'd seen enough earlier when helping to turn the woman.

"Those are telltale signs of hemlock poisoning, as is a musty aroma in the vomitus. She also appears to have endured several seizures, which is another side effect of hemlock poisoning. It is a painful death, and whoever inflicted upon her spent some time drawing it out for whatever nefarious reason." The surgeon looked upset. "It is most foul."

"I assure you, my husband and I will get to the bottom of this issue. We shall discover who murdered the woman, and you may rest easy knowing that."

The surgeon looked skeptical. "Forgive me, madam, but I do not see how you can accomplish such a thing. Mr. Trentworth has forbidden us to call the constable or send for Runners."

"Rest assured, we have some experience with these matters," said Lizzy briskly as she turned away from the man and the body. "I need to check on my mother and sister, Fitzwilliam. After that, I would like to speak to the women who were with Lady Longe yesterday. Perhaps they can offer some insight."

The surgeon still seemed unconvinced, but he said, "I suggest you make your inquiries discreetly, Mrs. Darcy, for Mr. Trentworth will not take kindly to your interference."

"Thank you for the advice, Mr. Hillgate." She nodded at him and turned fully away. Fitzwilliam offered his arm to accompany her from the room. He had a good memory for detail, so he navigated them out of the basement, back to the staff passageways, and into the main part of the hotel again.

"Are you sure this is a wise idea?" he asked as they walked up the stairs through the lobby, because he remembered her mother and sister had been given a room on the bottom floor at the back of the hotel.

"I am. If we do not investigate, the truth will remain unknown."

"Would that be so bad?" Even as he asked, he knew it would. For him, it would be an unsettling idea, and it would be practically intolerable for Lizzy, whose mind was already working at the puzzle and trying to unknot it.

She scowled up at him. "Of course it would, Fitzwilliam. I ask for your assistance in the matter, but I can manage alone if you prefer."

It was his turn to scowl at her. "That shall not be necessary, Mrs. Darcy," he said firmly. "I am your husband and will remain at your side during the investigation. I simply wanted to be sure you believe this is the correct course to take."

"I do, and I do not believe it will endanger any part of you, including your excessively vulnerable spot."

He shook his head at her, but a reluctant chuckle escaped him. "That is indeed reassuring, dear wife."

Moments later, they found Fanny and Kitty's room with the assistance of one of the maids. She knocked, and her mother opened the door seconds later, looking flustered, with a strange shine in her eyes. "Come in," she said, somewhere between strained and anxious. "You must tell us everything."

"Mama, allow the laudanum to work," said Kitty as she came forward, taking her mother by the arm and bringing her to a chair.

Fitzwilliam was impressed by how composed Kitty appeared, and he realized when she was away from Lydia, there was perhaps more to her than he had realized before.

There was a tray of tea waiting, and the pot was still relatively warm, so he poured himself and Lizzy a cup, realizing the strange gleam in Fanny's eyes came from the laudanum that had been liberally dosed in her cup, probably at Kitty's behest. It seemed like a sensible solution for the woman, for he could imagine how tightly wound she had been upon first reaching the room.

"What happened to the poor woman?" asked Fanny, her voice sounding wispy.

"She had a heart attack," said Fitzwilliam, conscious of Lizzy shooting a questioning look in his direction, but he avoided her gaze. "The manager pronounced it so." He left unspoken the disagreement by Mr. Hillgate, or the opinion it was hemlock that had done her in. He had no wish to spread scandal throughout the hotel, for if they were truly going to investigate, they needed as much of an element of surprise as possible on their side.

Lizzy must have reached the same conclusion, because she nodded a moment later. "It was dreadful. I am certain she was here to see to her health, but the waters did not work for her."

"Perhaps she'd not had a chance to visit the waters," said Kitty in an almost pragmatic voice. She sighed. "How sad."

"No doubt," said Lizzy. "How are you, Kitty?"

Kitty shrugged after a moment. "I feel strange. I have never seen someone dead before, but I did not know her, so I am not overly upset. Does that make me a terrible person?"

"I do not believe so," said Fitzwilliam before Lizzy could answer. "It was a distressing sight, but she did not die in an overly violent fashion, and passing is normal." Except when one was poisoned by hemlock. "It is natural, I am sure, to feel some trauma from the experience without mourning someone you did not know."

Kitty smiled slightly, looking relieved. "I am glad to hear that. Perhaps I simply have Lizzy's fortitude, and I shall join her in investigations."

"Not until you are older," said Lizzy. Then she smiled. "Of course, with any luck, we will never have another mystery to solve again."

Fitzwilliam felt like toasting that idea, but he wasn't entirely confident it was a possibility. Wherever they went, mystery seemed to follow them.

Chapter Five

Lizzy couldn't help admiring how Fitzwilliam had maintained his calm and managed to soothe both her mother and sister before they departed nearly forty minutes later. By that point, Fanny was on the edge of sleep, and Kitty was seeing to tucking her in. The laudanum would ensure her mother had a few peaceful hours, and she hoped Fanny would wake with her nerves in a much better state.

Kitty was handling the situation with aplomb, and Lizzy was proud of her. For a moment, she couldn't help imagining what fun it would be to investigate mysteries with all her sisters. They could be the Bennet Sister Runners—but she quickly shook her head at the notion. Lydia was far too flighty for such an endeavor, Mary was too pious and scholarly, and Jane was too sweet to handle this sort of thing. Even if it were just her and Kitty, they couldn't really call themselves the Bennet Sisters now, since she was Mrs. Darcy.

It was a silly flight of fancy anyway, for Lizzy had no intention of becoming a professional investigator. She might have a knack for this sort of thing, but it would be unseemly to seek out opportunities for investigation, and how would one find clients anyway? It was out of the question, but now that a murder had crossed her path, what choice did she have but to investigate when no one else was willing to do so? She and Fitzwilliam would tackle it as they had before, and though the situation was appalling, she was still invigorated by the idea.

She took his hand as they walked through the hotel in search of the woman who they soon learned by inquiring at the front desk was named Estella de Guille, and she was the niece of Lady Longe. She seemed like the most logical place to start, but they had yet to find her.

Suddenly compelled, she blurted out, "Have I told you today how much I love you, Fitzwilliam?"

He frowned down at her. "I have already agreed to assist you."

She rolled her eyes at him. "I am simply moved to tell you again. You have been most patient with my family and their unexpected arrival." She shuddered. "I do not know what my mother thinks sometimes. How could she assume it would be all right to join us on our honeymoon? That Papa did not speak up and point it out to her..." She trailed off with another shake of her head.

"Perhaps he tried, but your mother still did not understand the inappropriateness of it."

She snorted. "More likely, she was obstinately determined to come along anyway despite anyone else's voice of reason. She can be so stubborn at times." As she spoke, she was aware of his lips twitching, and she glared up at him. "Do not dare make that comparison."

He appeared to be striving for innocence. "What comparison, dearest wife?"

She wasn't fooled by his innocent tone. "You are about to compare me to my mother. That is a harsh offense, and I am uncertain I can forgive it."

He seemed like he might laugh for a moment, but then his lips settled down and stopped spasming. "Of course, Lizzy. You are nothing like your mother."

She nodded her head. "Quite right." Even as she agreed, she had to doubt that slightly though. While she and her mother were vastly different people, and their outlooks were completely separate, leading them both to find the other perplexing puzzles, there was some truth that she was stubborn like her mother. Her father could be intractable when he dug in on something as well, so she came by the trait naturally, though she was aware it wasn't always one of her most attractive features.

"They are here now, and we must deal with it, but I suspect it might not matter so much."

She frowned. "You do not think my mother and sister might have a prohibitive effect on our honeymoon?"

One side of his mouth tipped slightly upward as he gave her a half-smile. "I shall find it no more of an intrusion than a murder investigation, my love."

She grumbled under her breath as she nodded, accepting the wisdom of his words. "I suppose I should offer to not investigate. Is that what you want me to do, Fitzwilliam?"

He shook his head quickly. "I am not going to tell you what you can or cannot do, and I shall not try to bend you to my will. I could no more expect you to walk away from this investigation than I could expect your mother to be able to take tea with the queen and leave a favorable impression. You are who you are, and the person you are is exactly whom I love." As he said that, he paused, turning so she was facing him. He bent his head and kissed her on the nose gently. "You are indeed the love of my life, Elizabeth Darcy, and I will not stand in the way of your investigation."

She was unable to help herself as she reached up and put her hands around his face, bringing his mouth a little lower so she could kiss him properly. They exchanged a sweet kiss before she pulled back slightly and said, "I shall be happy to have your support. I know of no one quite so well-qualified to be my assistant."

He chuckled as he stepped back, putting his arm around her waist before taking her arm in a more polite fashion. She was unbothered by the lapse in decorum, for she enjoyed having him hold her too much to worry overly about it.

"You do have a way of putting me in my place, love."

She nodded up at him. "Quite right," she said too sweetly before they started walking again.

It felt like they had walked over most of the hotel before they finally found the woman they both recognized from the day before, who had been assuring her aunt that luncheon would soon be the new normal among Regency families. She was in the games room, the one reserved for women, and she was playing a round of whist with a group of ladies.

Lizzy didn't want to disturb her while she was in the midst of her game, so she pretended to take an interest in billiards. If the women found Mr. Darcy's presence alarming, none of them said anything or even bothered to look at him. She spent the next few minutes having him teach her how to arrange the two balls and hit them with the mace, intrigued by the game.

When the game broke up, Lizzy handed Fitzwilliam the mace and walked over to Estella, hoping to get her to open up. "May we speak with you, Miss de Guille?" As she asked, she looked closer, noticing the woman's swollen eyes and reddish sclera that indicated she had spent some time crying. Lizzy had questioned her ability to play a game under the circumstances, but now she realized perhaps it had been a distraction from the young woman's grief.

"I suppose it is about my aunt?" Her voice was slightly nasally, likely as a consequence of weeping.

"Yes. I take it someone has told you...?" She trailed off delicately.

Miss de Guille nodded. "I have been informed. I take it you must be the guests who found her?" The woman had a slightly grating tone, though she didn't appear to be irritated by Lizzy's approach. Perhaps her throat was irritated from sobbing.

Moved by compassion, Lizzy nodded as she resisted the urge to reach out to touch Miss de Guille's hand. "I was hoping you might answer some questions about your aunt for us."

She arched her brow, looking puzzled before she glanced at Fitzwilliam and then looked more closely at Lizzy. "Excuse me, but who are you to be asking questions?"

"Suffice to say, we have some experience with this sort of thing," said Lizzy in a vague fashion. "What did Mr. Trentworth tell you about your aunt's death?"

She frowned. "He said she had a heart attack."

Lizzy's lips clamped. "He could have at least told you the truth, since you are her relative."

Those words got the young woman's attention, and she fully looked at Lizzy for a long moment. "What do you mean, the truth?"

"The surgeon who examined her believes she was poisoned with hemlock."

The other woman scowled. "My aunt was not suicidal, I assure you. She'd been feeling under the weather more so than usual of late, so she was desperately hoping to find a cure here in the waters."

"He did not believe she was suicidal. He thought she had been poisoned over a period of days, or perhaps even weeks."

"What led him to that conclusion?" asked the woman as she crossed her arms over her chest, radiating her rejection of the theory.

"There were some physical characteristics. If they will not be distressing, I can list them for you, or you can accept a vaguer description and suffice to say the surgeon felt confident in his diagnosis."

After a moment, the woman nodded. "Very well. Why did Mr. Trentworth tell me it was a heart attack?"

Fitzwilliam stepped forward then, taking a seat at the table beside Lizzy, and she was glad to have his presence. He put his hand on her lap under the table, and she took it, squeezing lightly.

"Mr. Trentworth wishes to preserve the integrity of the hotel and avert a scandal. That is far more important to him than the truth."

"Whereas, we are far more interested in the truth," said Lizzy firmly. "If your aunt was murdered, and the surgeon believes she was, someone should have to pay for that. Do you not agree?" As she asked the question, she carefully evaluated the young blonde woman across from her.

Estella blinked for a minute, and then tears trailed from her green eyes. "I can scarcely believe someone would try to kill my aunt."

"Was she beloved by everyone?" asked Lizzy.

That startled a short laugh from Miss de Guille, though she quickly stifled it, and more tears streamed down her face. "Hardly, Miss..."

"Mrs. Darcy," said Lizzy.

The other woman nodded. "It was the very opposite, for Fern de Guille was generally an unpleasant, bitter woman. She found fault with everything, particularly if one tried to go against her. It was difficult to mollify her, to be blunt, and I got tired of trying. I do not remember the number of times she threatened to disinherit me if I did not fall in line."

"Do you believe she was going to go through with the threat?" asked Lizzy as suspicions started to rise.

Either Miss de Guille felt no fear at the possibility, or she didn't realize it might make her a suspect if it were true. "She had been more serious of late, but that was because she wanted me to marry her dead husband's nephew. Marcus Gladstone is milquetoast, and the idea of being married to him is frankly unbearable. I bluntly told my aunt not two weeks ago that if she felt compelled to disinherit me, she must do as she wished, but I would not comply with that request."

"Do you believe she made moves to do so?" asked Fitzwilliam.

Lizzy listened avidly for her response, though she tried to appear as though she was just casually interested.

"Perhaps." Miss de Guille shrugged. "I admit, I would live a much more comfortable life if I inherited my aunt's possessions and wealth, but my parents left me adequately cared for as well, so even if I never married, I could live a modest, independent life. I found that prospect much more appealing than marrying Mr. Gladstone."

"Of course, if she has not changed her will, you will inherit everything now," said Lizzy in what she hoped was a neutral tone.

Miss de Guille smoothed her dress as she stood up. "That is true as well, but if you are implying I killed my aunt to get her money, I fear you are not going to be a very good investigator after all. That could not be farther from the truth, but if you do wish to waste your time on the endeavor, you shall find no obstruction from me."

"How reassuring," said Lizzy. "In that case, do you mind if we interview the other woman who was with you at lunch yesterday?"

"Not at all. That is Mrs. Robinson, and she was my aunt's companion. You might also be interested in interviewing her abigail, Victoria. The girl is probably in our suite." She nodded to both of them. "I wish you good day, and believe it or not, I do hope you find the truth of what happened to my aunt. She was dreadfully hard to like, but I did love her nonetheless."

With those words, the elegant young woman swept from the game room, leaving Lizzy following her with her gaze for a moment before she looked at her husband. "What do you make of that?"

"She is either unburdened by guilt or fear, or she is a superb actress. Of course, we cannot rule her out just yet, but she seems an unlikely suspect, does she not?"

Lizzy nodded, slightly disconcerted. "She does seem to be the one with the strongest motivation though. If her aunt was truly about to disinherit her, it seems likely she would have been motivated to do everything she could to keep her inheritance."

"Yet she claims to have enough of an inheritance from her family to keep her in modest means. I can think of at least one other woman who would rather live modestly than marry someone she did not love."

"You are thinking of Anne," said Lizzy confidently.

Fitzwilliam surprised her by laughing. "That is true too, but I was thinking of you, my love. Would you rather not have lived a life of drudgery than marry Mr. Collins?"

Lizzy blinked at the conclusion, but she quickly nodded. "Most certainly, that would have been a far preferable fate. I see your point, but we cannot rule her out yet."

"Yes, I agree."

Chapter Six

Though Miss de Guille had not shared the suite number with them, it was simple enough to persuade a maid to help them. They knocked on the door, and it was opened some minutes later, but not by the unknown abigail. Instead, it was the other woman who had sat at the table yesterday. She frowned. "May I help you?"

"Have you heard what has happened to Lady Longe?" asked Lizzy.

The woman nodded, looking upset. "It is a dreadful occurrence."

"We have spoken with Miss de Guille, and she indicated she is amenable to us interviewing you." She kept her tone firm and compelling, wanting to present it as something Mrs. Robinson must accept.

The other woman frowned for a moment, but she stepped back to open the door. At first, Lizzy thought she was much younger, but as she passed by, she saw the first beginnings of crow's feet at the corner of her eyes and just a slight bit of furrowing at her forehead as well. Surely, Mrs. Robinson must be closer to forty than thirty as she'd originally imagined.

When Fitzwilliam had passed through as well, Mrs. Robinson closed and locked the door. "What is it you wish to know?"

"Perhaps we could sit and discuss it in a civilized fashion?" asked Fitzwilliam.

After a moment, Mrs. Robinson nodded and rang the bell. It didn't take long for a staff member to arrive at their door, and she said, "Bring us a pot of tea please." After dealing with that, she turned and joined them in the salon that was part of the suite, taking a seat in a wingback. "What is it that Miss de Guille has agreed to exactly?"

"What cause of death were you given for Lady Longe?" asked Fitzwilliam.

"The manager said it was a heart attack," said Mrs. Robinson with a wince. "She had been complaining of not feeling well, and her complaints had escalated of late, but the apothecary had never mentioned her heart before. Most distressing."

"It is also a lie," said Lizzy with deliberate calculation, wanting to shock the woman, hoping she revealed something in her response.

Mrs. Robinson jerked, though her expression didn't reveal anything terribly helpful. "I beg your pardon?"

"The manager is lying to obscure the truth of your employer's death, Mrs. Robinson. The surgeon believes she was poisoned with hemlock."

Mrs. Robinson flinched. "Surely not? Who would want to kill Lady Long? No, I am certain your physician is mistaken."

"He is not our physician," said Fitzwilliam in a hard tone. "He is a surgeon employed by the hotel, and he was the one who reached the conclusion. Mr. Trentworth chose to override the truth."

"Simply put, we are not prepared to accept that," said Lizzy with what she hoped was serene confidences as there was a knock at the door. They had to wait for Mrs. Robinson to fetch the tray from the hotel staff and returned to them, and Lizzy didn't speak again until she had a cup of tea and a biscuit moments later. "How did you find working for Lady Longe?"

Mrs. Robinson grimaced. "She was difficult and demanding, but she had a kindness to her as well. She had exacting standards, but as long as you could meet them, she could be a generous employer. She pays a full ten pounds more per annum than my last employer did. Or, she di..." She trailed off, looking overwhelmed for a moment. Mrs. Robinson paused to take a handkerchief from her pocket and dab her face, paying special attention to under her eyes before continuing. "I suppose I shall have to find a new employer now, which is a daunting prospect. Truly, though she was a difficult woman, I was quite fond of her."

"Do you know anything of her plans to disinherit her niece?" asked William.

Her eyes widened, and she looked down at her tea. "I should not speak out of turn, sir, particularly since Miss de Guille will be the one providing my letter of reference."

"We shall be as discreet as possible, but we need this information to ensure justice for your employer, whom you adored," said Lizzy with a gentle smile.

After a moment, Mrs. Robinson nodded again. "I see your point. She has a solicitor by the name of Chastain, and normally, he visits once or twice a year to discuss her business matters, but I had seen him three times in the last month or so. He and Lady Longe would secret themselves in the former Lord Longe's study and did so for a few hours each time. I confess, I was dreadfully curious..." She trailed off as she blushed, looking down. "I..."

"You perhaps listened at the door?" asked Lizzy gently.

Her blush deepened, and she nodded. "I did, though I am embarrassed to admit it." She looked up, appearing earnest. "I was afraid perhaps Mr. Chastain was giving her bad advice or steering her in the direction of naming himself as her heir. There is nothing particularly untrustworthy about him, but I have lived long enough in the world to know not everyone can be trusted."

Lizzy nodded, having seen her fair share of that over the last several months.

"I was relieved to hear he did not appear to be swindling her, but he was most assuredly helping her rewrite her will. She had removed Miss de Guille from it the last I heard, though I do not think Lady Longe got around to signing the changes in her will before her illness escalated, and she decided to come to Bath in hopes of finding a cure quickly."

"She became so ill rather suddenly?" asked Lizzy.

Mrs. Robinson nodded. "Of course, her health was declining steadily over the years, for she was an older woman. She was sixty-eight, and she used to say she didn't have very many years left, but she intended to make the most of them. The apothecary was a frequent visitor, and Mr. Seaton was concerned about her. He had been to Darby Park frequently for the last week or so. I believe he was the one who suggested she come take in the waters here at Bath when she started to feel drastically ill."

"Did you notice a change in her mental faculties?" asked Fitzwilliam as he shifted in the chair beside Lizzy. His hand brushed against hers in a reassuring fashion as he did so.

"I...perhaps I did. I thought maybe it was just because she was in such pain, for her stomach was bothering her dreadfully, and she was having certain indelicacies related to that, but I must admit, her thought processes seemed a little scattered even before last night's dramatic spectacle. I had never seen Lady Longe behave in such a fashion before, and it was disturbing."

"What happened after she left the dining room?" asked Lizzy.

"Miss de Guille and I brought her back to the room, and we assisted her in keeping calm while her abigail dressed her in nightclothes. Victoria gave her a dose of the medicine Mr. Seaton had prescribed, and Miss de Guille also insisted we add a dose of laudanum for her, hoping to help her rest easily until we could see the hotel's surgeon this morning. When we woke, she was already gone, and though we looked discreetly, we had not found sign of her before Mr. Trentworth delivered the cruel news."

"Do you know where Victoria is?" asked Fitzwilliam. "That is her abigail, is it not?"

Mrs. Robinson nodded. "Indeed, but I do not know where she went. She was most distraught, and I believe she frantically fled the suite. I did not find it overly strange at the time, assuming she was grieving, but..." She trailed off, biting her lip.

"Yes?" prompted Lizzy after moment.

"It is just perhaps suspicious. That, and..." Once more, she trailed off.

It was maddening, and Lizzy wanted to reach over and shake the woman to get a straight answer. "Please tell us everything you know. It is our best chance to find out who murdered Lady Longe."

At the word *murdered*, Mrs. Robinson flinched again. "Of course." She cleared her throat and set her saucer and cup on the tray. "Lady Longe yelled at her something fiercely last week, for Victoria had accidentally scorched silk stays while she was ironing them. She never should have ironed silk like that, and the lady was understandably upset by her doing so. Victoria should know such a basic thing, and it is not the first time I have heard Lady Longe complain about her lack of skills. She even went so far as to speculate that perhaps Victoria had fabricated her references, and I fear the girl might have been on the verge of being discharged from Lady Longe's employment."

"That hardly seems like a good enough reason to murder someone," said Fitzwilliam.

Lizzy shook her head, understanding why he was necessarily somewhat clueless about the idea. "You might not comprehend, Fitzwilliam, but for an employee turned out without a letter of reference, it can be almost impossible to find another position that is respectable. To obtain a position often requires the endorsement of another trusted employee, and that typically only works for your first job. A lack of reference can mean the difference between a respectable profession and a very much less respectable one." She left it at that.

He frowned. "I see. I did not realize it was such a grievous situation for a young woman to find herself in. Do you believe it might have led to murder, Mrs. Robinson? Does Victoria have the proper temperament?"

Mrs. Robinson shrugged. "I do not know her well, for she has only been in Lady Longe's employment for a few months, and I fear it is impossible to truly know someone's heart inside and out, no matter how close you believe you might be to them."

It wasn't much help as far as answers went, but Lizzy nodded. Mrs. Robinson seemed to be struggling to get through the rest of the day, and she was done with her questions for now. She shared a glance with Fitzwilliam, asking without words if he was finished as well. When he nodded, she took his hand before standing up. "Thank you very much for your time, Mrs. Robinson. I assume you will be staying a while longer if we need to speak with you again?"

"I suppose we are at Miss de Guille's mercy for that decision, Mrs. Darcy. She is now the one making all the financial decisions, and if she does not immediately turn me out because she does not require a companion, I will of course be deferring to her wishes. If I am present and you need to question me again, I shall make myself available to you."

"That is all we ask for now." With a brisk nod, Lizzy started walking toward the door, with Fitzwilliam right behind her. She appreciated having him at her back, for there was no one else in the world she trusted so well to protect and support her.

Chapter Seven

"I must insist you get some real food, Lizzy. We have been at this for a few hours, and you will not do well in your investigation if your senses are not sharp." Fitzwilliam said the words in a persuasive fashion as he nudged Lizzy toward the dining room, feeling more than peckish himself.

Her stomach rumbling precluded her from disagreeing, though he suspected she wanted to. She was inspired by the investigation and clearly wanted to see it through. He could read her well, and it was obvious she was keyed up to find Victoria and get her accounting of everything. That was something that could wait until they had lunch though, and he firmly steered her in the right direction.

Surprisingly, she put up no resistance, and they were soon seated at a table near the door, though inside instead of outside this time. It was a hotter day, but there were still people outside. Two of them in particular caught his attention when he heard a familiar voice that he quickly identified as belonging to Estella de Guille.

Lizzy tensed as well, indicating she had noticed the voice too, and they both turned slightly in their seats, wanting to get a better view. There was a large plant and glass wall in the way, but with the patio door open, he could make out enough to see with whom Estella sat. It was a woman he was unfamiliar with, but she wore a serviceable plain gray gown. Her hair was confined in a mobcap, and she seemed to be out of her element.

"Do calm down, Victoria," said Miss de Guille in a firm voice. "Your behavior might suggest you are guilty."

"Never, Miss de Guille," said the young woman in a soft voice. "I would never harm your aunt."

"I did not say you had," said the lady in an impatient tone. "I simply want you to be on your guard about what you say to outsiders. I do not believe you killed my aunt, but it is well-known that she was displeased with your service. I would not like to see you implicated for a murder you did not commit."

Victoria burst into tears then. "You are so kind, Miss de Guille."

"It is not kindness, but practicality. You know my secrets, Victoria, and I know yours. Therefore, we are each incentivized to keep our confidences, are we not?" There was a note of warning in the woman's tone.

Fitzwilliam frowned as he heard it, looking over to Lizzy, who was leaning so far forward in her chair that he was afraid it might tip over at any moment. She was clearly glued to every word.

"Of... Of course, Miss de Guille. I shall be judicious with what I share. Should we depart Bath?"

"If we returned to Somerset-Upon-Marsh now, it might cause more questions to arise. I wish you to speak with the infernal busybodies, but do not share too much. That is all I ask."

"After everything you have done for me, I shall certainly abide by your wishes, Miss de Guille."

When Fitzwilliam heard the sound of chairs scraping, he quickly got to his feet and rushed over to Lizzy, setting her chair right and pulling her into his arms. She looked like she was going to protest, but he didn't allow it. He simply bundled her against him and rushed to the opposite side of the room, near the fountain pumping out water. He took a glass and filled it, keeping his back to the ladies as they exited the room a moment later. Then he turned to offer the glass to Lizzy, though she scowled. With a shrug, he took a sip instead and then grimaced. "It tastes terrible."

"It is full of minerals that are supposed to be good for you, but that does not mean it will taste good." She put her hands on her hips. "What were you doing, Mr. Darcy?"

He grinned. "Oh, dear. I am back to Mr. Darcy now. You must be displeased with me."

Her glare deepened. "I am displeased that you allowed our suspects to get away."

He had to resist the urge to laugh, knowing she would not take it well. "I do not believe they have gone anywhere, aside from leaving the dining room. As you overheard, Miss de Guille instructed the abigail to speak with us, but not freely. I am certain we shall have a chance to do so later, but now we know we cannot trust everything she says. Further, they do not know that we know that. If they had seen us, it might have been a disaster."

Lizzy opened her mouth, looking like she might argue for a minute, but then she leaned back and nodded, her hands gradually dropping from her hips. "I suppose you are right. I was simply caught up in the fervor of the moment, and it did not occur to me to obscure my identity. I hope we did not miss anything else of importance."

"I doubt they were intending to say much more, particularly if it could be overheard. We know now that they have secrets, and they are both guarding them for the other. That will either make them more resilient, or perhaps it will provide some leverage if one of them is in a stronger position than the other. Indeed, I believe we have learned more to help our investigation in the last five minutes than we did the entire time we spoke with Miss de Guille or Mrs. Robinson."

Lizzy frowned. "Perhaps you are right." She moved closer, taking the glass from him. She sipped it and then set it aside with a grimace of distaste. "Foul."

"It most certainly is. If that is the cure, I think perhaps I would prefer the disease."

"Do not know that it is good for gout?" She winked at him. "That is why Prinny is coming next week, or so the rumors say."

"With his habits, I suspect his ailments are far more prurient in origin." He frowned in distaste. "I am heartily glad we will be able to avoid interacting with him. I doubt he would notice us anyway, but I do not wish to have to share the same space with the man." Fitzwilliam scowled, finding Prince George IV to be a most disagreeable scoundrel.

"Do you believe she influenced Mrs. Robinson's interview as well, Fitzwilliam?"

He put his arm around her waist and nudged her gently forward so they could walk as they talked. "I do not think so. At least, it did not seem as blatant. I suspect whatever secrets Miss Victoria and Miss de Guille share might have been inadvertently confided. Surely, Miss de Guille has not taken both servants into her confidence, though perhaps she has some sort of leverage over Mrs. Robinson. I do not believe we can take any of their interviews at face value, but we were never naïve enough to do so anyway, were we?"

She shook her head. "It is true you are an appalling judge of character at times, but I concur with you. We can certainly not trust any of the three of them."

He scowled at his wife as he led her toward the staircase, almost surprised she didn't ask what his intention was. "When have I ever been a poor judge of character?"

Lizzy was clearly startled, and she let out a laugh that was louder than she probably intended. She clamped her hand over her mouth for a moment until she contained her mirth, though she was still smiling when her hand fell away. "You believed my sister was a gold digger."

"I thought perhaps she was motivated by the need for security and spurred on by your mother. I never believed she was a gold digger." He said the word staunchly.

She snorted. "Of course not. What about poor Lord Aumley?"

He scowled. "The young viscount could still very well be a rake."

"I highly doubt that, but he is most certainly not a murderer. You would not have thought he were if you were not jealous." She seemed to enjoy that.

"I believe I had good reason to feel jealous. I thought you were on the verge of making a terrible mistake with him."

"Why ever would I do that when I was on the verge of making a terrible mistake with you instead?" said Lizzy with a wink.

"Minx," he said as he increased their pace up the stairs.

Her smile widened. "Wherever are you taking me, Mr. Darcy?"

"To our suite, Mrs. Darcy. I find myself in need of reassurance that you are fully committed to me and do not believe you have made a mistake." He intended the words to come out in a light, teasing fashion, but they sounded far more serious than he'd planned.

She stumbled for a moment, and they paused in the middle of the staircase. "I was simply teasing, Fitzwilliam. I have not made a mistake, and I shall never feel that way." She took his hand. "I love you, dear husband."

"I love you too, dear wife, but I still need reassurance. Perhaps you could spend some time proving it to me before we tackle interviewing the abigail?"

Her gaze sparkled, and she nodded with enthusiasm. "I do believe that is a sound plan, Fitzwilliam."

Chapter Eight

Lizzy was staring up at the ceiling, lazily drawing abstract figures on Fitzwilliam's chest with her finger. Their exchange had certainly led to a satisfactory conclusion, and she was so sated she could barely force herself to think about anything else.

"Are you happy, Lizzy?" he asked unexpectedly as his hand captured hers, removing it from his chest to fold between his fingers.

She turned slightly to look at him, frowning. "Of course I am. What we have is more than I ever imagined it could be, Fitzwilliam."

He let out a harsh exhale. "I confess, I am still concerned at times that you will decide you have made a mistake."

Her frown deepened. "Why would I ever feel like I made a mistake?" The concept made no sense to her, for she had been fully committed and decided on the course of action before she married Fitzwilliam after his proposal at Pemberley.

He turned her hand over so the back was lying on his stomach, and he started tracing the lines on her palm. "I suppose it is just a peculiar insecurity of my own. I feel like I have loved you far longer than you loved me, and I suppose I worry you will change your mind."

Lizzy pulled her hand away and sat up, changing positions so she could loom over him. "You probably do not intend to offend me, but you are suggesting I am flighty and capricious, husband. I am not, I assure you. I concede you have probably loved me longer than I loved you, but now that I do love you, it is fully and with my whole heart. There is nothing that will change that."

He closed his eyes, and he appeared relieved. "I am sorry if I sound like I am doubting you. It was not my intention to offend you."

She laid a hand on his cheek, waiting until he opened his brown eyes before speaking again. "I always want you to tell me what you are thinking and feeling. I can promise I shall not change my mind, but if the fears arise, you must tell me so you can be assuaged."

After a moment, her husband smiled, and he seemed completely relaxed again. That changed a moment later, because he stiffened when she said, "It seems obvious that we must have a chance to search Lady Longe's possessions. While they are off to dinner, I can dress as a servant and slip into the room to search. There is unlikely to be anyone there."

He was back to scowling again. "You most certainly shall not, Elizabeth Darcy. Your days of dressing as a man are over."

Lizzy cocked a brow at him. "Are they?"

He cleared his throat. "I do hope they are over. At this particular moment, the need for a disguise seems unwarranted. After all, we can merely slip into her room during the dinner hour."

Her eyes lit up with excitement. "You shall assist me?"

"I live to assist you, my dear. Do not worry. I do not consider myself your equal in this task." His eyes were gleaming as he teased her.

She grinned in response. "Excellent. How shall we gain access? I do not suppose you know how to bypass a lock?"

He frowned. "I cannot say that is a skill I have ever acquired. To be honest, considering your somewhat dubious upbringing and lack of parental oversight, I confess myself bewildered that it is a skill you lack."

Lizzy took his slight mocking in stride, already considering the practicality of it. "You are absolutely right, Mr. Darcy."

He frowned. "Right about what?"

"I have been severely neglecting part of my skillset. Once we are finished with our travels, I shall apprentice with a locksmith to learn everything I can, so I am no longer wanting in such a situation."

He looked genuinely astounded. "Lizzy, I was not serious. You do not need to be schooled in how to break locks."

She grasped his hand in her enthusiasm, nodding earnestly. "Oh, but I do. Think how useful such a skill would be right this minute, or rather, at the dinner hour? We would not have to rely on others to gain access to places we need to be."

He shook his head. "I fear my anxiety for you will be the death of me, Lizzy. It must be by design."

She quirked a brow. "What is?"

"Your serious stubbornness and intention to lay a course intended to shorten my lifespan significantly from fretting. No doubt, you have designs on inheriting all of Pemberley."

He was being melodramatic, and she rolled her eyes. "You have unearthed my nefarious plot, dear husband. Once I have you out of the way, I should bring in a team of gently bred women who would like to become investigators and school them in everything I have learned." She giggled at his sour look. "I confess, I much prefer to have you around, and not just for obvious reasons."

He cocked a brow, looking cautious. "What obvious reasons?"

"You are quite a good assistant when it comes investigating, of course." She trailed her hand gently down his stomach. "You do have wealth and power that you wield quite efficiently when need be, but you never abuse it."

Her hand drifted lower, and his breathing grew more ragged. "Then there are the less tangible benefits," she said as she lightly squeezed him in a teasing fashion and made him draw in a deep breath. Before he could get too worked up, she removed her hand and smiled at him. "All of that in spite of your exceedingly tender spot."

"Lizzy," he said with a note of warning.

She smiled at him and patted him on the chest in a soothing fashion. "We really must get up and prepare. I suspect we might be able to figure out how to unlock the door by practicing on our own." As she started to climb out of bed, she looked down at his hand clamped around her wrist. "Is there something else?"

"Yes. One does not start something without finishing it." As he spoke, he pulled her down on top of him, grasping her face before giving her a long kiss. When they broke apart, he said, "For tonight, I will bribe the front desk clerk to give us the key. That means we have extra time."

She had no trouble inferring how he wanted to spend the time, and she was most agreeable. Casting a quick glance at the clock on the mantle, she smiled. "Indeed we do. We have ample time, in fact."

THEY WAITED A FEW MINUTES past the beginning of the dinner hour before using the key Fitzwilliam had obtained for the outrageous sum of a one-pound note to slip into Lady Longe's room. Fitzwilliam secured the key in his pocket, locking the door behind him, and Lizzy was already moving through the suite. She went straight to the armoire, opening the doors to examine the deceased lady's possessions. As she sorted through an assortment of dresses, undergarments, and jewelry, it quickly became obvious there was little to hold an answer there. Fitzwilliam was examining the escritoire, and after finishing her task, she went to him. "Have you found anything of use?"

He sighed. "I have not. At least, nothing that is clearly of use. I fear, I do not know for what we should be searching."

She nodded her agreement. "I suspect we would know what if we saw it, but perhaps nothing stands out because nothing helpful exists. There must have been a reason why someone wanted her dead other than just her being an unpleasant sort."

"I concur, for if one murdered just because someone is unpleasant, Lady Catherine would have been deceased long ago."

She tapped him lightly on the arm. "Fitzwilliam, I am surprised you would make a joke about that." Despite her tone of censure, she couldn't help her lips twitching, and she ended up chuckling. "You are quite terrible, husband."

He grinned in a charming fashion. "You do not deny the truth of the charge."

Lizzy shrugged a shoulder. "How could I? It is quite accurate, I am certain." She frowned, looking around. "I fear this was a waste of our time."

"Undoubtedly," he said softly as he reached into his pocket for the key. "I suppose we must return this and regroup."

She started to nod her agreement, but both of them froze when the door to the adjoining room suddenly opened, revealing a young woman standing there. She wore the drab gray of service, and though she was startled, she quickly appeared on the verge of screaming.

"Please, do not cry out for help. We mean no harm," said Lizzy quickly. Keeping her hands in front of her and moving slowly, she approached the young woman at a cautious pace. "We are looking into the death of Lady Longe. You must be Victoria?"

After a moment, the woman nodded, though she still looked afraid. "Please, I did not know what was in it." Her voice was familiar, and Lizzy recognized it from eavesdropping on Miss de Guille when she had her conversation with Victoria.

Lizzy stiffened at the words, even though she kept her tone gentle. "What was in what, Victoria?"

Her hands were trembling, and Lizzy was uncertain when she started to depart the room. She thought she might be running, but she didn't feel like she could reach out and try to hold the young woman against her will. When the maid disappeared into the smaller room set aside for the abigail, she looked back at Fitzwilliam, who seemed equally puzzled. Neither of them knew how to proceed, but before they could debate on whether to follow her, Victoria reemerged.

She held something in her hand, which she extended to Lizzy. "The apothecary said to give her ever-increasing doses to counteract her convulsions and abdominal pain, and I followed it to the letter, though it seemed to me she was gettin' worse with each dose. I asked Lady Longe if she should discontinue the medication, and she about boxed me ears for me impertinence. She thought I was daring to be above my station and considered meself smarter than the apothecary. I swear, miss, I did not. I was just trusting me own eyes."

"I can certainly respect that," said Lizzy. She looked at the vial in her hand, and it was an oil amber substance. She cautiously unscrewed the top and wrinkled her nose at the musty scent. It was unpleasant, to say the least, and she immediately wanted to speak to Mr. Hillgate. He had been able to identify the smell of hemlock from Lady Longe's vomitus, so it was likely he would recognize the scent if it were what tainted the vial. "You say an apothecary gave you this?" At Victoria's nod, she said, "Do you know where we might find him?"

"Of course, miss. It was given to her by Mr. Seaton at Somerset-Upon-Marsh, where we live."

"Where might that be?" asked Mr. Darcy as he stepped forward.

"It is but twelve-mile up the road, Mr. Darcy. I reckon a carriage could take you there in less than two hours."

"To your knowledge, nothing has been changed about this vial? It is still what the apothecary gave her?" asked Lizzy.

Victoria nodded once more, seeming completely sincere. "Yes, miss, though I did not have it in me possession. It was here in the lady's room, and I only had it in me room after..." She trailed off, looking pale. "I was afraid someone would think I had poisoned the lady, though I did not."

For a moment, Lizzy was tempted to ask her about what she'd overheard when Victoria was discussing the shared secret with Estella, but she decided to keep those questions in reserve for now. At the moment, Victoria was still an ally, and she viewed Lizzy and

Fitzwilliam as people she could trust. Lizzy didn't want to upset that fragile balance, though she had not yet decided if it was safe enough to trust Victoria's word.

They left the hotel room moments later, stopping by the front desk to drop off the key and ask the clerk where they might find Mr. Hillgate this time of evening. He directed them to the infirmary, where the surgeon had a room at the back. When they arrived, they had to wait for a moment after tapping on the locked door.

Mr. Hillgate opened it himself a few minutes later, and he looked slightly disheveled. "Pardon my appearance, but I did not anticipate seeing more patients this late." He opened the door, fiddling with his cravat. "What brings you..." He trailed off as he recognized them. "Mr. and Mrs. Darcy, I do hope you are not here with another dead body."

"No, but we perhaps might have the cause of the first one." She reached into her reticule, removing the vial and handing it to the surgeon. "This is a medication given to Lady Longe by her apothecary in Somerset-Upon-Marsh. Do you recognize it as having hemlock?"

As she finished asking, he was unscrewing the vial. He took a deep breath and grimaced before putting the lid firmly on again. "Yes, it has the characteristic musty smell, with perhaps just the slightest underlay of parsnip. Hemlock is in the carrot family, but it is certainly not something one wants to eat."

"Would it be difficult to acquire hemlock?" asked Fitzwilliam.

The surgeon frowned for a moment. "Botany is not my specialty, but I believe it grows rampantly and naturally just about anywhere. In particular, water hemlock is common along bodies of water, as you would expect, and it is even more poisonous than the other variety of hemlock. I believe if one knew what they were looking for, they could find it easily enough, particularly since it has white flowers and distinctive purple spots on its stems."

"Thank you, Mr. Hillgate," said Lizzy. She took the vial from him again, not wanting to let it out of her sight until they had finished their investigation. They took their partings from the surgeon and left moments later, returning to the room to plan.

Chapter Nine

With Mr. Trentworth's cooperation, Fitzwilliam had arranged for them to have a carriage the next morning at their disposal. It was a rental, and there was no driver. It was just a phaeton with two horses, but it would see to their needs efficiently. They could surely reach Somerset-Upon-Marsh within two hours at the pace the horses set, and it was a fine day for riding, though a little hot. Lizzy had her parasol, and he appreciated that it shielded his eyes as well as they embarked on their mission.

"Someone wishes to harm her, so they give her hemlock. Apparently, it would seem either they wanted Lady Longe to suffer, or they wanted her to pass when they were not nearby, so they gave her small doses and gradually increased them over a few days, understanding the neurological and respiratory effects the poison would have."

Fitzwilliam nodded as Lizzy spoke, recognizing she was simply walking through the steps, which seemed to be part of her process.

"The apothecary is the obvious answer, for he was the one tasked with making the medication. However, we have not met him yet, so perhaps he has no motivation. I suppose it would be easy enough to tamper with the vial if one were determined."

"Particularly if it were in an oily base. I am assuming hemlock infusion would also be created in oil." He enjoyed the way she smiled at him, clearly liking his intelligence. What should've been a patronizing look instead made him feel like he was ten feet tall coming from Lizzy.

"That is a good point. One must assume creating hemlock infusion would take a while. I know it takes Mrs. Hill several weeks to get a proper garlic infusion into the oils she uses at the house."

"Did you spend much time in the kitchen?" he asked in a teasing voice.

Lizzy surprised him by nodding. "Hill is quite a fascinating woman, and she knows all sorts of bits and bobs that are not necessarily related to the culinary arts. Most of all, she was a calming influence when I was a child, as were our nurses. Mama was always high-strung, and so I naturally gravitated toward people who were not in their temperament."

He felt a moment of sadness for her, especially when he considered how calm and soothing his own mother had been. Anne Darcy had never suffered from the mysterious ailment of "nerves," to his relief.

"I recall watching Hill perform the process for infusing garlic in her oils once. She said it had to be in a dark place for several weeks. That suggests either our poisoner routinely keeps hemlock oil on hand, where they have easy access to it, or they had been planning to kill her for a while."

He nodded his agreement with her assessment. "We know Miss de Guille and the maid are conspiring about something."

She nodded. "They are not necessarily conspiring, but they do share a secret. Whether that secret is relevant or could ruin someone enough to kill for remains to be seen."

"I concede that point." The horses were well-trained, so he was able to hold the reins in one hand. He relaxed the other and reached over to take her hand, enjoying the splendid moment, and all the more because they had managed to slip out of the hotel before running into Fanny and Kitty and being sidetracked or cornered, or having to explain why they must leave so early.

He couldn't imagine how unpleasant the day would be with one or both of them along chattering incessantly. Most assuredly, they would not have been able to freely discuss the investigation.

"Mrs. Robinson seem to have no real issue with her, though she admitted the woman could be crotchety. It sounds like Lady Longe wasn't particularly likable, but does that make one want to murder her?" She shook her head. "Clearly not, for as we established, a great many people would already be murdered if that were enough to provoke most people to the act. There must have been a reason or catalyst. Miss de Guille still seems like our best suspect, for she was about to be disinherited."

"I agree, but we should not be too attached to the theory, lest we overlook the truth if it is different from what we are expecting."

She squeezed his hand. "That is indeed a wise point. I can think of no one else with whom I would rather investigate such matters, my love."

He grinned. "I cannot help contrasting this with how you felt the first time we ever worked together when Wickham was robbing Meryton." He couldn't help grimacing as he said Wickham's name. The man was waiting at Newgate for deportation to Australia, though his trial had not begun yet.

Fitzwilliam had every intention of attending when it was finally his turn before the judge, because he intended to do everything in his power to see the man deported. He did not wish Wickham to hang, but he also wanted the man out of the country before he could cause more mischief.

"We must carefully scrutinize the apothecary, for he is likely to have both the medications needed to create whatever was put in the vial and perhaps access to hemlock. If it is commonly grown as Mr. Hillgate suspects, it seems like it could be easily harvested, and surely, he would have the knowledge of how to prepare an infusion or decoction."

"I concur." There was little more to say on the matter, so their topic of conversation turned to Pemberley, and what Lizzy would like to see there. They discussed the new stables that were currently being built, along with slight changes she wanted to make to the interior.

He had no objection to any change she might want to undertake, and when she suggested it was time to pack up his father's study, he was certain it was because she thought he wanted to remove Wickham's picture. There was truth to that, so he made no objection when Lizzy asked if she could turn the room into her own personal office and library. It did not surprise him that she wanted to have such a fixed space to herself. It did prompt him to ask though, "Were you at all serious when you alluded to continuing investigating?"

She hesitated for a half-second, her head cocked slightly to the side. "I confess, I do have a talent for. I do not try to be immodest, for I am equally surprised as anyone else. It is invigorating to try to put together all the pieces of the puzzle and find the correct answer, particularly if someone else has overlooked it."

"Such as Constable Walters," he joked.

She shot him a repressive look. "The man would overlook anything, so I would hardly consider that a challenge. No, I cannot see setting up shop as Mrs. Darcy, investigator, but nor will I shy away if the opportunity presents itself."

"I pray that it does not again after this experience," said Fitzwilliam firmly. "For my part, I am content to settle into wedded bliss and live boringly for the rest of our lives."

Lizzy shook her head as she clicked her tongue. "Even if we never find another crime to investigate, love, I cannot imagine our life together will be boring."

He squeezed her hand. "No, I am certain you are correct. Life with you will never be boring, Lizzy." He couldn't help recalling at her visit to Pemberley and how she had dressed as a young serving boy so she could accompany him into the tavern to investigate the murder of his stablemaster.

He was soon chuckling as he recalled her ridiculous attempt at a mustache created from cutting off an inch of her hair and stealing gum paste from the kitchen to apply it. It had fooled no one, nor had her attempts at a masculine walk. Before he knew it, he was guffawing and had to pass the reins to her.

She gave him a bewildered look, not asking what had amused him so until he could breathe again. He used his handkerchief to wipe his cheeks, having laughed so hard that tears flowed down his face. When he was removed from the situation, no longer irritated by her machinations, he could appreciate how truly entertaining it had been.

"What is it?" she asked as she handed back the reins.

"I was just remembering Mr. Bennet, with his ridiculous gum paste mustache and silly walk. No, life will never be boring with you, Lizzy. Of that I am certain."

She harrumphed at him, but her lips were twitching slightly too, indicating she shared his amusement, however reluctantly, since her own actions had provoked it.

SOMERSET-UPON-MARSH was a small village, much as he had expected. They arrived a little more than two hours later, having kept a reasonable pace for the horses, and he stopped the first person he saw on the street, asking, "Where might I find the apothecary?"

"Mr. Seaton is one street over. You cannot miss the sign," said the older man as he bowed his head in a respectful fashion before hurrying on. Following the directions led them quickly to the apothecary's door, easily recognized by the sign above that identified *Seaton's Apothecary*.

He stepped down first and then used his hands to assist Lizzy down, lifting her away from the muddy area and onto a paver brick. He joined her, scraping his shoes on the metal scraper by the door before they walked into the office.

A small bell on the door rang, announcing their presence, and a man around thirty emerged from the back. He was a pale, thin fellow, but handsome enough, Darcy supposed. He seemed earnest, and he gave them both a reassuring smile. "How may I assist you today? I do not recognize you, so I take it one of you has fallen ill while traveling?" His gaze moved to Lizzy. "Perhaps you require something for motion sickness?"

Lizzy shook her head. "We are here about Lady Longe. I assume you know her?"

Mr. Seaton's expression tightened. "I am familiar with Lady Longe. I have treated her upon occasion. Surely, she has not registered a complaint about me? I have never done anything but try to please the woman." He made it sound like that was an impossible task.

"Lady Longe is dead," said Fitzwilliam abruptly. He made no attempt to shroud the news in delicacy, wanting to see Mr. Seaton's reaction.

The man blanched, and then he started to pale. "H... How?"

"She was poisoned with hemlock." Lizzy was the one to reveal that, slipping her hand into her reticule to retrieve the vial. "The surgeon at the hotel has confirmed hemlock was in the solution. Is this the vial you prepared for her, Mr. Seaton?"

He moved slightly closer, and Fitzwilliam put himself between them in a protective fashion. Lizzy annoyed him by stepping around and holding out her hand, keeping the vial on her palm. When Mr. Seaton would've reached for it, she closed her hand and pulled back. "Do you recognize it, Mr. Seaton?" she asked again.

He was scowling now. "The vial, certainly, but it did not have hemlock. It was a homeopathic preparation I designed because she was having fits and more severe stomach issues than usual. The digestion issue was a prolonged condition she had complained about for years.

I see it sometimes. It is as though the patient has an irritable digestive system. There is no call for hemlock in it. When I do use hemlock as a homeopathic preparation, the flowers and roots are rendered only beneficial via homeopathic preparation methods. The result is conium, and it is for restless minds. The treatment would not have been useful for Lady Longe, and it is prepared as an alcohol extract before being succussed in water. It is not in an oil base."

"You did not add hemlock then?" asked Lizzy.

He shook his head. "I did not, and I resent the implication."

"Tell me, would it be easy enough to acquire around here?" asked Fitzwilliam softly. "We have heard it is particularly prevalent near bodies of water. Am I right in assuming there is a marsh nearby, due to the name of the town?"

"There is, but I have not spent much time there, not since I was a boy, and it is not where I would acquire hemlock—which I have not needed for a patient in several years. If neither of you require treatment, I am afraid I must ask you to leave. Patients will be coming in soon, and I have no wish for them to overhear the specious allegations against me." With a dignified air, the man marched to the door and held it open for them. "I am certain you can see yourselves out."

He thought about arguing, but Lizzy seemed content to leave, so he followed her lead. Once they were outside with the door closed behind them, he frowned. "I expected you to get slightly more aggressive with the questioning, Lizzy."

She smiled. "I believe it was obvious he did not intend to cooperate, but there is still a possibility we might find someone who can help shed light on the situation."

He frowned. "Such as?"

"If you recall, Mrs. Robinson mentioned Lady Longe had met with her solicitor three times recently. Somerset-Upon-Marsh is so small that if they have one solicitor, he is likely to service everyone in the area. It is possible they might have to send to somewhere else for a solicitor, which might make it more difficult to track hers down, but I suggest we ask around and see if there is a solicitor here."

He nodded his agreement, and soon enough, they had found a person who directed them to Mr. Chastain's office. It was a small building in the middle of the village, and it appeared neatly kept. There was a hand-lettered sign outside hanging from a post, and someone had been diligent with burning the letters precisely into the wood.

Everything about the place was meticulous and tidy, and Fitzwilliam was unsurprised to find Mr. Chastain was of a similar nature. He had every hair carefully arranged and oiled into place, his cravat was as perfect as if he'd had a valet assisting him with tying the Gastronome's complicated configuration, and his bespoke suit was perfectly fitted to him. He was a man who was likely to have everything in order, and Fitzwilliam hoped he had an organized and tidy mind as well.

He led them to a seat across from his desk and offered tea. Once they all had a cup in hand, he sat down at his desk and leaned forward. "How may I assist you? You are not from the area, I take it?"

"No, we are visiting at Bath," said Lizzy.

"I fear we bring bad news," said Fitzwilliam as he added milk to his tea. "There has been a death at the hotel."

The solicitor frowned. "Was it Lady Longe?" He must've realized how startled Fitzwilliam was, because he nodded at him. "It is an easy deduction to make, for why else would you travel all this way? The lady headed there in hopes it would improve the sudden onset of whatever mysterious illness had afflicted her, and she went so abruptly that she did not have time to sign the new will she asked for that changed her beneficiary."

"Yes, disinheriting Miss de Guille. Would you be shocked to learn the surgeon at the hotel believes she was poisoned?" asked Lizzy in a neutral tone.

The solicitor frowned, his slender brows drawing together as he did so, and he set aside his cup. "I suppose I would not be terribly shocked, though I truly cannot see her niece murdering her, if that is your implication. Miss Estella had a singular gift of being able to tolerate Lady Longe. It was a talent few of us possessed in great quantity."

"She does seem unpopular," said Fitzwilliam.

"Certainly. She was my client from the time I inherited the practice from my father, but I confess that calling upon her for every task sent me into a prolonged state of dread, and I always endeavored to speed along business as hastily as possible. Not to speak ill of the dead, but Lady Longe was not a warm and affable woman. She was incredibly exacting, and what she was doing to her poor niece seemed criminal to me."

Fitzwilliam frowned as he shifted slightly, setting aside his cup and saucer as well. "Those are strong words, Mr. Chastain. Would you care to enlighten us?"

"The girl refused to marry the man her aunt had selected for her." His lips clamped for a moment as he seemed to consider something. "Rumors have a way of abounding, especially in a particularly small village like ours, and they suggested Miss Estella had a different suitor, one her aunt would consider far beneath her."

"Do you know who?" asked Lizzy.

The solicitor shrugged. "I am afraid I do not. I try to ignore gossip as much as possible, but inevitably, you hear some here and there. Regardless of why, it was obvious Miss Estella was refusing to fall in line. I believe the first two times Lady Longe sent for me, it was merely to intimidate her niece with the action, but the third time, she was violently angry. She ranted for quite a while at the girl's intractability, insisting she was ready to go ahead with rewriting her will. I got the impression she had recently learned the identity of Miss Estella's suitor and was appalled."

"You agreed to do so despite your objections to her actions?" asked Lizzy.

He shrugged. "Of course. She is my client, and I am obligated to do as she bid. I drafted it for her, and then I had only to come back here, finish the finer details, and I was to deliver it to her in two days' time for her signature. When I showed up at Darby Park, the butler told me she had abruptly departed for Bath, hoping to find a treatment for her illness."

"And to whom did she leave her wealth in the revised, unsigned will?" asked Fitzwilliam.

Mr. Chastain hesitated for a moment before sighing. "I suppose there is no harm in revealing it now, for the will was never signed, so nothing is legally binding. She chose to leave it all to the vicarage instead. It was to be held in trust, with a portion allotted each year for whatever vicar happened to be in charge. Of course, there were myriad conditions placed upon it, including the moral integrity of the clergyman. He had to be selected from her choice of traits for however long the trust lasted."

"It does sound rather like the controlling impression we have gained of Lady Longe," said Lizzy with a slight upward lift of her lips.

The solicitor gave a small smile too. "As I said, she had high standards and was very exacting in them. She expected full and complete compliance, or retaliation was swift."

"Do you know if Miss de Guille had heard about being disinherited?" asked Fitzwilliam.

For the first time, Mr. Chastain seemed uneasy. He cleared his throat and looked away. "Perhaps I should not divulge..."

"As you said, it hardly matters now, Mr. Chastain," said Lizzy in a persuasive voice. "We are simply trying to find the truth of the matter."

Fitzwilliam wondered if he would ask why they were involved, and why they cared, but apparently, he hadn't given it a thought. After a moment, he said, "To be honest, I warned her myself. I sent a letter to her the day after I had been summoned for the third time, this time instructed to rewrite the will. It was a succinct letter, and there was nothing particularly sensitive about it, but I did warn her that if she had any inclination to change her mind and fall in line with her aunt's wishes, she should do so quickly, before the lady had a chance to sign the will."

"She had warning then," said Lizzy, obviously thinking deeply.

He frowned. "Please do not believe that Miss Estella could ever do something so vile as to kill her aunt though. She is a kind and gentle soul, and she did not deserve the fate befalling her."

Fitzwilliam looked at Lizzy, who nodded as she set aside her teacup. "Thank you for your time, Mr. Chastain." He got to his feet, offering Lizzy his arm, which she took. The solicitor escorted them to the exit, closing the door behind them, and they continued to walk serenely to the phaeton.

Chapter Ten

Lizzy waited on discussion until they had departed Somerset-Upon-Marsh, stopping at an inn for lunch before doing so. Now that they were on the road back to Bath, and it was just the two of them, she said, "Am I imagining that Mr. Chastain seemed to be in love with Miss de Guille?"

Fitzwilliam hesitated for a moment and then shrugged. "I cannot say for certain, but even if he does not love her in that way, he clearly respects and likes her. He felt she was being dealt an injustice by her aunt."

"One could have concern for an acquaintance, but I do not think one would murder for such a tepid relationship." She tipped her head as she considered it. "What if Mr. Chastain was feeling particularly protective of Miss de Guille? Somehow, he arranged for the poison to appear in the vial, perhaps even paying Mr. Seaton to prepare it despite the apothecary's protestations to the contrary. The dosage would have been slowly increased, and it was conceivable that she might feel the need to adjourn to Bath."

Fitzwilliam shook his head. "I am do not think that makes sense, Lizzy. He would have no reason to suspect she might go to Bath when she got quite ill. Most people would be more likely to take to their bed and send either for the apothecary or perhaps to London for a skilled physician. Someone of Lady Longe's wealth could have easily done so, but she did not. Instead, she chose Bath, which is not an entirely irrational choice, but perhaps it wasn't the soundest one she could make either. If she were already feeling the neurological effects of the hemlock, it might have influenced her to the crazy choice, but I do not think the solicitor could have relied upon her making that decision."

Lizzy nodded, conceding the point. "I admit, that is a stretch, and I suppose there was no reason for someone to specifically want her to die in Bath, save it is a geographic distance from her home and might lessen suspicion on someone. Perhaps she went to Bath with encouragement from someone close to her? If Miss de Guille was involved in conspiring, she might've been the one to suggest the trip herself."

"Perhaps Mr. Chastain is the person with whom Miss de Guille is involved, and the one to whom Lady Longe objected, but he seemed genuinely surprised to hear of the lady's death."

Lizzy sighed, realizing he was correct. "He was not surprised to hear about the possibility she had been poisoned though."

"I can see why. She does appear to have few admirers among her circle."

She felt a touch of sadness for the older woman, though she suspected whatever dislike Lady Longe prompted had been cultivated by her own actions. They did not excuse murdering her though. "If it was not Mr. Chastain, then whom?"

"We are back to Mr. Seaton, who was the one to prepare the vial, and he would have easily been able to add hemlock to it."

After a moment, Fitzwilliam drew the carriage to a stop, and she frowned. "What is it?"

"It is something I noticed passing earlier, but I did not take time to show you then." He dismounted the phaeton and lifted his arms to help her down before leading her into a field. They had to walk through a few feet of weeds before she saw a spindly plant with lacy white flowers. Bending closer, she could see purple-red spots on the stalk and stems, and she said, "This is hemlock." She had never seen it before, but it certainly matched the description Mr. Hillgate had provided.

"I believe it is too. If there is a patch here, there is likely even more closer to Somerset-Upon-Marsh. Mr. Seaton would certainly have the knowledge of how to prepare it thanks to his training. He even told us how it was done."

"But why would he murder Lady Longe?"

"Perhaps he was the one involved with Miss de Guille. It still makes sense that she might've been the one to instigate the murder plot upon learning she had been disinherited or was about to be. After all, Mr. Chastain had warned her, and it seems likely she could have increased Lady Longe's dosage of hemlock to spur her illness to accelerate. She might have even been the one to suggest her aunt go to Bath, or she might have been working around the lady's decision to do so. I feel we cannot rule out Miss de Guille, Victoria, or Mr. Seaton."

Lizzy walked with Fitzwilliam back to the phaeton, accepting his assistance to take her seat again before he joined her. "I believe you are correct. When we reach the hotel again, I would very much like to speak with Miss de Guille once more."

"I am certain we can arrange that. Perhaps it will be most illuminating."

Lizzy certainly hoped so, as they were on the verge of solving the mystery, but there was still something missing. She found it vexing that she didn't have all the pieces just yet, and she couldn't see what knowledge she lacked to make it all fit together into a neat answer. She longed for that moment, both for justice for Lady Longe, and also because it was quite gratifying to be the one to find a solution.

THEY RETURNED TO THE hotel a couple of hours later, just in time for tea. They entered the dining room, and Lizzy was pleased to see Miss de Guille sitting by herself at a corner table. They approached, and she smiled. "May we join you, Miss de Guille?" Without waiting for acceptance, she took a seat, and Fitzwilliam hastily held the chair for her before assisting her to push it forward. Then he sat down beside her.

"To be honest, I would rather be alone," said Miss de Guille in a starched tone. "I am in mourning." She was certainly dressed the part in her mourning weeds, a black veil and black walking dress, but she didn't seem overly upset.

"We shall not tarry for long," and Lizzy in a confident voice. "We have been to Somerset-Upon-Marsh."

Miss de Guille stiffened. "I beg your pardon?"

"We went there to have a talk with the apothecary and Mr. Chastain. Did he not warn you about your aunt's plan to disinherit you?"

The other woman stiffened and nodded just once. "He was kind enough to do so."

"When we last spoke with you, you left it far vaguer than that, acknowledging it was a possibility, but you did not seem to possess any special knowledge that it was indeed a probability." Fitzwilliam made that observation as he poured himself a cup of tea.

"It is hardly your business."

"We must concede that," said Lizzy with a hint of regret. "Still, we are involved, and we have learned something of interest. Mr. Chastain warned you, and the hemlock given to your aunt came from a vial prepared by the apothecary."

She flinched then. "Edward would never do such a thing." Then she paled, clamping a hand over her lips for a second before it fell to her lap. "Mr. Seaton is a professional."

"Is he the man you love?" asked Lizzy in a gentle tone. "There is no point in denying you are involved with someone beneath your station, someone of whom your aunt disapproved enough to disinherit you when you refused to give him up to marry another. Was it Mr. Seaton?" She still thought it could be Mr. Chastain, but he had the kind of attitude that suggested he regarded her from afar rather than in an intimate fashion.

Miss de Guille's expression crumpled, and she reached for a handkerchief as she slipped a hand under the veil and used it to dab her face. "Edward is a good man. Kind, warm, and solid. My aunt could not see that, for she could not look past the fact he came from common stock, and he and his father were tradesmen. She deemed him not good enough, and she insisted I would marry the man she'd chosen for me, or she would disinherit me. I would have nowhere in the world to go, but she underestimated my fortitude."

She straightened her shoulders and sniffed delicately before removing the handkerchief. "I admit, I was not looking forward to living more humbly, but between Edward's living as an apothecary and the inheritance left by my parents, we will get by. I would truly rather scrub floors than marry the man she has picked for me. I barely know him, and what I do know is unpleasant. Most importantly, I do not love him, and nor do I believe I could ever grow to do so."

"Especially when you love another," said Lizzy softly, conveying her understanding. She recalled how she had striven to develop a *tendre* for Lord Aumley, but her heart had been set on Fitzwilliam even then, though her mind hadn't accepted that just yet.

"Yes, and I love Edward so much. I told my aunt this, and she was so much worse just a few hours later. I thought I must have brought on her latest flareup with my insistence on maintaining the right to choose whom I married." She sniffled again. "When she insisted on coming to Bath, I came with her, though she was still angry with me. However, she was also too sick to really focus on it, and her mental state deteriorated in a matter of hours. I still cannot believe Edward would be the one to poison her. I reject that assumption, and I insist there must be another explanation."

"What about Mr. Chastain?" asked Fitzwilliam.

Miss de Guille frowned. "What of him?"

"Do you think he has a *tendre* for you? If so, would he be protective enough to kill for you?"

Her eyes widened, and after a moment, she looked like she was going to laugh. "Oh, dear, no. Mr. Chastain is a lovely man, and we played together often as children. We maintain a friendship to this day, but he is not at all romantically interested in me, I can assure you."

Lizzy frowned. "He seemed quite protective and tender toward you."

"He is like a brother to me, and he would never fall secretly in love with me, I assure you."

Lizzy shook her head. "You cannot be sure if he did not tell you. Do you suppose his love for you would be strong enough to spur him to kill to protect your inheritance?"

She did giggle then, though she looked stricken by the sound and quickly clamped her handkerchief over her mouth. "I insist Mr. Chastain does not love me, and he does not have the temperament required to kill anyone. As I said, he is like a brother to me." She cleared her throat and leaned closer, dropping her voice to a discreet whisper. "If I'd had a brother, he would be far more likely to gain Mr. Chastain's intimate affections than I would, if you take my meaning?"

Lizzy's eyes widened as she sat back while Fitzwilliam gasped lightly. She was certain she was intuiting the meaning correctly. When she looked at her husband, she was certain of it, because he seemed shocked.

"Of course, I expect your complete discretion, for he means no harm to anyone, and it should not matter to anyone whom he loves." She said the words in a defiant, angry fashion that was far more passionate than any emotion she'd displayed toward her aunt.

To Lizzy's way of thinking, it still made Miss de Guille a strong suspect, but she no longer believed Mr. Chastain had been involved in any fashion aside from warning his old friend. That didn't strike off Miss de Guille and Mr. Seaton from the suspects list though.

SHE SUPPOSED IT WAS inevitable she would have to interact with her mother and sister again, and they found themselves dining together later at the dining room. Her mother appeared quite recovered from the shock of discovering the body yesterday, and Kitty seemed to have mostly forgotten about it as well.

She was too busy discussing the charming young brothers she'd met that afternoon in the garden, who were visiting with their grandfather. Lizzy resisted the urge to remind her sister not to flirt or do anything inappropriate, feeling more secure that her sister would display slightly more common sense since Lydia wasn't around to help lead her astray.

"Of course, talk still centers around the scandal of the death. Can you imagine, coming all this way and then still dying of a heart attack?" Fanny clicked her tongue, as if she disapproved of Lady Longe making the trip and having the bad manners to die before the water could heal her.

"It is a spot of bother," said Darcy in an indulgent voice. "It makes one wonder why she bothered to come here at all. If she knew she was going to die, would it not have been more polite to stay home to do it?"

Lizzy had to smother her laugh at his teasing tone, not at all surprised when her mother failed to pick up any of the quiet mocking in it. It was all gently delivered of course, for Lizzy's entertainment and not to injure her mother's feelings.

"I suppose one does not know they are going to have a heart attack, my dear son," said Fanny. "I have no doubt, she would have done the decent thing and stayed home to die if she had realized it was an imminent possibility."

Fitzwilliam had stiffened slightly when she called him her son, but he was now relaxed again. "I have no doubt she had faultless manners and would not wish to inconvenience anyone with her death."

"But if she did not, you would have no further need to investigate," said Kitty in a bright tone. "There has been some good to come from it."

Fanny frowned. "Kitty, do not be ridiculous. Lizzy is done with all that nonsense. As Mrs. Darcy, she could hardly undertake such things as murder investigations." She stated the words oppressively as she glared at Lizzy, practically daring her to contradict them.

"I fear I must retire," said Lizzy in a serious voice, doing her best to maintain her expression of earnestness. "We all know Mr. Darcy has exacting criteria, and if I fail to fall in line with them, it is quite likely he will lower me from wife to scullery maid. I must spend every moment of my existence ensuring he is pleased with my performance or risk being banished."

Fanny seemed shocked. "Lizzy, that is not at all like you. You must truly love him."

Kitty was giggling, though she was doing a good job of hiding it in her napkin. "It is a wonder you have time to think anything of yourself, dear sister, when you are so preoccupied with ensuring Mr. Darcy's existence is the pinnacle of perfection."

Lizzy couldn't help it. She reached for her napkin and started laughing too, burying her face in it.

Fanny finally seemed to realize they were teasing her, and she frowned at them. "I would expect such behavior from Elizabeth, but not from you, Kitty. You are behaving too much like your father."

Kitty grinned unabashedly, and Lizzy continued to chuckle into her napkin. Fitzwilliam seemed to be having some trouble controlling his amusement as well, for he dabbed repeatedly at his mouth until he finally sat up straight, and his lips were in a reasonably tight line. "You should be ashamed of yourselves, ladies. Your mother is only thinking of my comfort, which we all know is paramount. After all, I would hate to demote you, Lizzy."

She pretended to be suitably chastened as she bent her head, but she was still snickering. "Yes, Fitzwilliam," she said in a subservient voice that was far too sweet to be believed by anyone except Fanny.

Her mother shook her head, looking more amazed. "You are a marvel, Fitzwilliam, at how you can mold and shape Lizzy. It is a task I have failed at for many a year, I assure you."

Lizzy couldn't help thinking to herself that Fitzwilliam had a secret weapon. Not only did he love her and motivate her to want to make him happy, he was completely devoted to making her happy as well. It didn't hurt that her husband was also a skilled lover, a recent discovery she'd been happy to make and was eager to rediscover at every opportunity.

Chapter Eleven

The next morning, Fitzwilliam and Lizzy went to speak with Mr. Trentworth, telling him what they had learned. He still adamantly wanted to cling to the idea that it was only a heart attack, and the surgeon was overselling it to make an impression on the Prince Regent, who would arrive the next week, but Fitzwilliam refused to allow that to continue.

"We must involve the local constabulary. Your village constable must bring Mr. Seaton here. I tell you this as a courtesy, not to gain your permission, Mr. Trentworth. I understand the need for discretion and wanting to avoid scandal tainting the hotel, but this is a murder investigation, and the truth must be found. I cannot allow you to stand in the way of it."

Mr. Trentworth drew himself up, looking like he wanted to argue for a moment, but as Fitzwilliam stared down at him, his shoulders slumped, and he crumpled into his seat. "Very well, Mr. Darcy, but I tell you now that if these actions bring harm to the hotel, it is you I have to hold accountable. It will be your fault if jobs are lost and no guests return."

"I accept that liability," said Fitzwilliam with a touch of seriousness he had to force. He hardly thought it would be such a dire thing, even if guests did learn someone had been murdered at the hotel. From what he had observed of humanity in general, it was more likely to prompt the arrival of a certain group of visitors than to send them away, for people had an innately macabre curiosity, at least a great many of them, and he doubted there would be a shortage of people who would want to see where the victim had died.

After dealing with Mr. Trentworth, they called upon Mr. Johnson, who was the village constable. He seemed a sight more competent than Mr. Walters, and equally competent to Mr. Smith at Lambton, and he quickly agreed to the task of fetching Mr. Seaton to bring him there.

With nothing left to do but wait, he and Lizzy returned to the bathing room, both separating to go to the segregated pools. When he emerged sometime later, he felt more relaxed and invigorated, and Lizzy appeared to be in a similar state when she joined him after they met outside the changing rooms.

"It does seem to be taking forever for the constable to return," said Lizzy.

He shook his head. "It has been not but an hour, my dear. You are simply impatient."

She heaved a sigh, but she didn't argue. "That I am. I do wish we could bring him much faster."

"At most, the horses can only go eight miles per hour, so it will be some time yet. I suggest we walk in the garden."

"Very well. I would like to enjoy some part of our honeymoon as a honeymoon, rather than a murder investigation or a chance to entertain my mama and sister."

He tucked her hand into the crook of his arm, and they started walking. Soon enough, they were outside enjoying the meticulously planned English garden. Everything was in its proper place, and it somewhat reminded him of the grounds of Rosings Park. He couldn't help recalling the night they had sneaked out to catch Mr. Collins in the act of blackmailing his cousin, and he was glad that ugliness had passed. "I have a suggestion, my love."

She paused and tilted her head. "Yes?"

"After we have wrapped up this unpleasant business, and our stay here has ended, I would like to take you elsewhere to continue our honeymoon. The continent is out, of course, and sailing to the colonies or elsewhere would be far too long of a trip, but perhaps we could go to Brighton, or maybe into Scotland. I would like to have a stretch of uninterrupted time with you."

She seemed eager for the idea, but she hesitated. "What about Pemberley? Can they do without your presence for a time, especially with the stable being built?"

"Wainwright is proving to be reasonably competent, and he has his father, who is only in semi-retirement, if he needs help. I feel like spending at least a month away."

She smiled again. "In that case, I enthusiastically agree, but with one caveat."

He arched a brow. "What might that be?"

"We should tell no one, especially my mother, where we are going next." She grinned at him.

He smiled in return. "I accept that condition, though I do believe perhaps we should leave word with Bingley and your sister, or with my cousin, Richard. Someone should know where we are, but assuredly, it should not be your mother."

"Most assuredly not."

THEY HAD LOITERED ABOUT the constable's office, so they saw his coach approaching hours later. He stopped in front of the building, got down from the driver's seat and walked over to the carriage, opening the door to reveal Mr. Seaton, who looked decidedly reluctant to be there. His hands were in cuffs, and they had been secured to a bar inside the carriage. It was clear Mr. Johnson had thought ahead and had prepared for his role far more seriously than Mr. Walters ever had.

They followed him and Mr. Seaton inside as Mr. Johnson marched him up the steps and into the building, placing him in a seat near the reception desk.

"I am certain you know why you are here," said Lizzy.

Mr. Seaton glared at her. "You believe I poisoned the old biddy. I did not, and that is all I will say on the matter."

"What we would really would like to know is if you and Miss de Guille were acting together, or if you were doing these actions to protect her. We already know you were both involved in the plot," said Fitzwilliam with confidence.

Lizzy's eyes widened, for she had not reached that firm conclusion, but she quickly realized Fitzwilliam was simply saying it in hopes of rattling some useful information from Mr. Seaton.

The man surged forward, but he didn't quite leave his seat at a warning look from Mr. Johnson. "I did not poison Lady Longe. Estella most certainly had nothing to do with it. Somehow, she managed to retain affection for the unpleasant old hag."

"It is clear you have no respect for her," said Lizzy with a hint of reproof.

He snorted. "Indeed, I did not, but you would be hard-pressed to find many who did. She was unpleasant and demanding. The woman had a list of people as long as my arm who disliked her. You can hardly accuse me of murder just because I hated her."

"Truly, I can understand your hatred. She was trying to keep you from Miss de Guille, and more than that, she was trying to force the woman you love into marrying someone else. It is understandable in such circumstances how you might be motivated to do something extreme to protect you and the woman you love," said Lizzy in a sympathetic tone.

He glared at her. "I did not kill her, and I did not add hemlock to the vial. Estella most certainly did not, but if you are determined to continue this line of inquiry and cling to your faulty assumptions, I will have no choice but to confess to protect Estella. I assure you, neither of us plotted against the old woman though. Estella had already accepted she was going to be disinherited even before Mr. Chastain sent word of the maneuver. We were making plans for her to leave Darby Park and come live with me. If you do not believe me, you can speak with the village vicar, with whom we had already registered our intent to marry. Our names will be read for the next three Sundays when they announce the banns, and then we can get married. All of this had taken place before Lady Longe fell ill so quickly."

Lizzy grimaced at the news, realizing the man was hardly likely to invoke the vicar as an alibi or source of proof if it weren't true. Very few vicars would've lied in such a position, particularly for congregation members who weren't in a position to offer financial incentive to do so. If they couldn't even afford the accelerated license that would allow them to marry in a week, let alone a special license, it seemed unlikely they could contribute the amount required to persuade a vicar with fixable morals to lie for them.

"I believe those are all the questions we have for now," said Fitzwilliam abruptly to Mr. Johnson. "Will you keep him locked up here for now?"

"Of course, Mr. Darcy. He is not yet cleared in the investigation."

THEY WERE REENTERING the hotel a few minutes later, having discussed the feasibility of Mr. Seaton still being their suspect in light of the plans he and Miss de Guille had made, when Mrs. Robinson approached them. She seemed distraught. "What progress have you made?" She asked the question more of Darcy than Lizzy.

He cleared his throat. "We have some solid leads. We believe Mr. Seaton might have been involved in creating the poison."

She frowned. "The apothecary? It does make sense. After all, I saw them together." She flushed, looking down. "It was most indiscreet, but they were being so blatant about it. What choice did I have but to tell Lady Longe?"

"Tell her what?" asked Lizzy.

"I saw Miss de Guille embracing a man not even a week past. I thought it must be Mr. Seaton, though they were some distance away when I saw them. I immediately told Lady Longe when next I saw her." Her voice took on a bitter edge. "I had expected some gratitude, not a chastisement to avoid gossip, though she seemed furious at the revelation. Lady Longe was always a difficult one to please."

She blinked then and looked around. "If you will excuse me..." She trailed off as she hurried away.

Fitzwilliam frowned at her as she rushed from them. "She is the one who betrayed Miss de Guille then."

"I suppose she thought she was doing the right thing, but it almost seemed like she expected to be rewarded, did it not?" asked Lizzy.

He nodded. "And she appeared bitter that she was not rewarded as expected. I suppose it was possible Lady Longe already knew."

"Undoubtedly, she had suspected it. I would venture she had not yet identified the man's identity until Mrs. Robinson's revelation, for that coincides roughly with when Lady Longe sent for Mr. Chastain for the third time." Lizzy's frown deepened. "I still feel like we are missing something."

He nodded his agreement. "I concur, but what?"

After a moment, she smiled. "Who always knows the goings-on in a household, Fitzwilliam?"

He frowned. "The master?"

She squeezed his arm even as she laughed at him. "I am certain you would like to believe that, but I think the answer is more basic than that. Below-stairs always knows what is happening above-stairs, and I suspect Victoria knows more than she has revealed. She is certainly sharing a secret with Miss de Guille, and I suppose it is time to extract it from her."

If Fitzwilliam felt like arguing—and he didn't—she gave him no opportunity to as she sped up the stairs, practically dragging him along with her. There was no need to drag though, for he was happy to follow her anywhere.

Chapter Twelve

They found Victoria in Lady Longe's suite. She was tidying up and packing things away when she let them in. It was obvious that was her task by the open trunks, some half-filled, and the items missing from the armoire.

"You have been busy," said Lizzy, hoping she had an unthreatening tone.

The maid nodded. "Yes, miss. Miss de Guille has instructed me to pack up everything and tells me we will be returning to Darby Park in the next day or two. She has agreed to keep me on as her lady's maid."

"There must be a relief. I suppose it has something to do with the secret you share?" asked Lizzy gently.

The maid's eyes widened, and she looked horrified for a moment. "I... What?"

Lizzy shook her head. "It is all right, Victoria, but we do know about the secret."

Victoria crumpled to the floor, looking like she might sob at any moment. "Who told you? Miss de Guille swore she would never tell anyone. Was it my cousin?"

"Who is your cousin?" asked Fitzwilliam.

"Mr. Seaton. He is the one I came to. He knew the rough life I lived, and how I was afraid of the man who had been selling me to others. He promised to help me, and Miss de Guille offered her help as well. She was the one who got me the job with Lady Longe. I do not know how she managed to do it, but she even got a notarized letter of reference."

"Mr. Chastain," said Lizzy speculatively, seeing Fitzwilliam nod out of the corner of her eye.

Victoria frowned. "The solicitor?"

"Never mind that. Is that the only secret? Do you have a secret about Miss de Guille?"

Victoria hesitated before shaking her head. "I cannot say."

"Cannot or will not?" Lizzy knelt on the floor beside her, placing a gentle hand on the woman's shoulder to reassure her. "We already know about Miss de Guille and her involvement with your cousin, Mr. Seaton. Was that the only secret between you and her, besides your past?"

Victoria started to sob, but she nodded. "Yes, miss."

Missus," said Fitzwilliam with emphasis. "Mrs. Darcy."

It seemed like a silly time to point it out then, but Lizzy imagined Fitzwilliam was somewhat sensitive to hearing her called just miss, since he seemed proud to call her his wife. She sent him a warm look as Victoria nodded again.

"Yes, Mr. Darcy," she said in a subdued tone. Then she looked at Lizzy. "Miss de Guille was trying to help me, and she never told me I must keep her secret, yet I cringed when I heard Mrs. Robinson telling Lady Longe. She quickly dismissed her companion, and then she spent the next half-hour venting her spleen about Mrs. Robinson's gossiping and threatening to bring scandal to Miss de Guille when Mrs. Robinson was doing far worse."

"What was far worse?" asked Fitzwilliam. He seemed to be trying to make himself smaller as he sat on the floor with them, his back against the bed. It was the most casual and unusual place to see him, and Lizzy was temporarily distracted by the gentleness of his manner and his attempts to put the other woman at ease. She couldn't resist the compulsion to reach out and take his hand as she smiled at him before focusing on Victoria again.

"Mrs. Robinson was carrying on with the coachman. I did not know that until Lady Longe revealed it. She also told me then she was planning to replace Mrs. Robinson in the near future, when she found a suitable candidate. She was going to turn out Mrs. Robinson without a reference. She said it was no more than she deserved and the lesson she deserved for having such loose morals, and so of course, I could not bear to even imagine telling her my secret."

"Did you warn Mrs. Robinson?" asked Lizzy.

Victoria shook her head. "I did not, for it was not me place. I thought about it, but Mrs. Robinson has never been particularly warm to me, or to anyone, that I can see, and so I did not feel I had any measure of loyalty to her. I suspect she knew though, or perhaps she was just planning to leave anyway, because I noticed Lady Longe started losing pieces of jewelry in the weeks before we left for Bath.

"It was only a necklace here or a pair of earrings there over the last few weeks, and though it escalated in the past few days, Lady Longe was becoming too ill to notice. I thought about saying something, but I was afraid she would blame me instead. She was never a very forgiving or openminded sort, but as her mind started to deteriorate over the past several days, she became what one might call paranoid."

"I can understand why you chose not to confide in her," said Lizzy.

"Thank you. I feared she would immediately dismiss me without a reference, and I did not know if I could handle the strain on me nerves of trying to find a new place with another fake letter of reference. I do not wish to be sent to prison for doin' so." Victoria looked like she might start crying again. "Will you be telling on me, Mrs. Darcy?"

"I shall do my very best to keep that information out of the investigation, Victoria." She squeezed her shoulder again and said, "Will you be all right here alone?"

"I will, Miss...Mrs. Darcy." She shot a cautious look at Fitzwilliam. "Do you know who has done this thing, Mrs. Darcy?"

"I have my suspicions. You been invaluable, and I will do my best to protect you as I promised, Victoria." Squaring her shoulders, she waited for Fitzwilliam to get to his feet, and after waiting another moment to ensure the maid wasn't going to fall apart, they left the room.

She was only a few feet in the hallway before she couldn't contain herself, and she turned to face Fitzwilliam. "We need to see Mrs. Robinson's room."

He seemed serene about the idea. "I agree, and I have an idea about how we might accomplish that."

TWO HOURS LATER, MR. Trentworth himself opened the room for them, though he looked pained to do so. "You will be brief?" he asked again, clearly needing the reassurance.

"We shall be finished with our search before Mr. Johnson is finished getting Mrs. Robinson's accounting of the events that led up to Lady Longe's murder."

Trentworth flinched at the word murder, and he paled further. "Yes, yes. See that you are." He didn't even try to stay to watch them. Apparently, he decided he wanted no part of what was to follow.

Lizzy immediately moved toward the armoire as Fitzwilliam went to the trunk at the foot of the bed. When he opened it, it was partially emptied, so his search wouldn't take as long. Lizzy turned her attention to the armoire, and at first, she found nothing of interest, save for an advert from the London paper.

There was a list of positions that were opening for ladies' companions, and she noticed the date was a couple of days before the one that seemed to herald the increasing severity and sharp turning point of Lady Longe's illness, which had prompted her quick departure to Bath. "She was looking for a new position. That confirms what Victoria said."

"That is not all," said Fitzwilliam in a solid voice as he stood up, closing the trunk and spreading out a small selection of books on it.

Lizzy moved closer, eyeing the titles. They all related to botany and herbal preparation. One was a small pamphlet she recognized that been sent throughout England to warn people of the most common types of poison and how to avoid them. As she read the brief pamphlet, it was a perfect how-to guide to find hemlock and properly identify it. It was written from the perspective of how to avoid using it or mistaking it for something benign like carrots or Queen Anne's lace, but it could also be used by someone who was a would-be murderer.

The botany books went into greater detail about it, and the herbal preparation book included information on how to prepare an infusion. Lizzy was confused though, because the books looked older and well-thumbed. Even the brochure looked like it had been weathered by age, so the woman must have had the information for a while.

"It appears she has had the knowledge for some time, but why?"

"She is a widow," said Fitzwilliam in a speculative voice. "I mean, if we assume she is being honest by referring to herself as Mrs. Robinson."

Lizzy frowned. "Do you think she poisoned her husband?"

He shrugged. "I cannot say with any degree of confidence, but it is a possibility that occurs to me. If she had used hemlock to solve her problems once before, it might seem like a logical solution, particularly if she had some remaining available to her."

She frowned, wondering if hemlock could lose potency over time. It seemed like it probably could but would likely still be strong enough to kill after a year or two. But would Mrs. Robinson have kept a supply after she'd accomplished her plan to kill her husband, if that was why she had it to start with? As Fitzwilliam said, perhaps she considered it a solution to any serious problems that might arise. "I would very much like to talk to her."

"As would I, but not without someone to ensure your safety."

Lizzy moved closer to him. "We need someone to overhear her confession."

He arched a brow. "You are confident in obtaining a confession then?"

"I believe I can. Still, the constable must be present to overhear, and she is unlikely to reveal such thoughts or actions in front of him. Indeed, you would probably have an inhibitive effect as well."

"I perhaps will agree to allow you to speak with her alone, but only if it is the illusion of being alone. I will not have you risking yourself in such a dangerous venture unless we have a very solid plan, love."

For a moment, Lizzy chafed at his attempt to impose a restriction upon her, but she quickly realized it came from concerned love for her. He didn't want to control her. He simply wanted to ensure she was safe. That he was willing to allow her to ostensibly approach Mrs. Robinson alone was a sign of his clear faith in her, and she nodded her agreement. "I have an idea."

Chapter Thirteen

Thanks to Mr. Trentworth's observation skills, which were surprisingly sharp considering how dull he was in general, they knew Mrs. Robinson liked to take a turn around the garden shortly before bedtime. That had been her pattern since arriving at the hotel, but Lizzy was nervous that she might deviate for some reason.

It was a relief when she heard footsteps approaching, and they sounded feminine. To be sure she was presenting a convincing picture, Lizzy bent forward on herself and started sobbing, burying her face against the gown covering her knees. She hid her face because she knew she wasn't producing real tears, but she hoped she was making a passably convincing sound of crying.

The footsteps drew closer, hesitating for a moment as she continued to sob. Lizzy wondered if her loud expression of sorrow would be off-putting rather than enough to spur Mrs. Robinson to approach. She considered toning down the sobs, but then she heard the steps continuing forward, picking up speed now.

A moment later, she was aware of a presence behind her. She slowly lifted her head, vigorously scrubbing at her face in hopes it would hide the fact she wasn't actually crying real tears.

"Mrs. Darcy?" asked Mrs. Robinson, her voice laden with concern. "Are you all right?"

"Mrs. Robinson. I did not know you were here. Forgive me for my display." She wiped her face again, scrubbing with her sleeves in hopes it would leave her face red. It certainly left the skin feeling somewhat raw.

"What troubles you, my dear?" She looked around before coming to sit by Lizzy. "Where is your husband, Mr. Darcy?"

"We had an argument. He said I was being insolent by talking back." Lizzy cupped her cheek, hoping she gave the implication he had struck her. "I have never seen him behave in such a fashion before."

Mrs. Robinson seemed angry. "They never show that side of themselves when they are courting you, Mrs. Darcy. You poor dear. This is the reality of being a married woman. There is no escape." She sounded bitter.

"Are all husbands this way?" asked Lizzy.

"I cannot say confidently, for I had only the one, but he was a most violent fellow." Mrs. Robinson's expression tightened, and she trembled for a moment. "It was on our honeymoon as well that he started showing his true signs. He accused me of flirting with a man, though I had done nothing of the sort. It was a few days before I could walk, and it was a lesson I never forgot. I do not believe I ever looked at another man for more than ten seconds until Mr. Robinson had passed."

Lizzy couldn't help the sympathy that shot through her. Even suspecting Mrs. Robinson was a murderer twice over, it was difficult not to feel compassion for her plight. "Have you looked at a man since then?"

For just a moment, Mrs. Robinson had a softening in her expression. "There was a man... He was a good enough man to make me think that maybe, just maybe, there are some decent men left in the world. Unfortunately, Lady Longe turned him out without reference, and we lost touch."

"What was her reason for doing such a terrible thing?" asked Lizzy softly, hoping she'd struck the right note to encourage confidence rather than cause Mrs. Robinson to pull away.

"I might have been. I think Lady Longe discovered we had a relationship, and she would not take kindly to that. A few masters are compassionate enough to allow people in service to marry and have a life of their own, but there was nothing terribly kind about Lady Longe, and she quickly dispatched the coachman, knowing he was easily replaced. After that, she was never quite the same with me either, and I knew my days were limited as she searched to find someone else to replace me."

"That must have been quite trying. Were you looking for a new position?"

The other lady nodded. "Of course, but I fully expected not to be able to find one without a good letter of reference, and I was certain she would turn me out the same way she had Thomas, in such an abrupt fashion. Had she not been reliant on assistance to get around even before she got so sick, I have no doubt she would have sacked me the same day she did Thomas." She sighed. "She was an unpleasant woman, and she enjoyed bringing strife and pain. It was only fitting that she got some in return."

"Did you have the hemlock left from Mr. Robinson?" asked Lizzy gently.

Mrs. Robinson stiffened. "I do not know what you mean."

"I assume you found a way to solve the problem of Mr. Robinson and create an escape. Perhaps if a young married woman has realized she has made a similar mistake, she might be able to obtain the same sort of solution."

Mrs. Robinson frowned. "Are you accusing me of poisoning my husband?" She sounded neutral to the idea.

"Accusing is a strong word, Mrs. Robinson. Perhaps I could substitute the word hopeful." She touched her cheek again, trying to look pensive. "Perhaps I have realized I have made a grave mistake and chosen the wrong man. I am looking for some hope. Is there a way to escape?"

"I suppose there is always a way, provided you are brave enough, girl. Your solution can be prepared in a matter of weeks, and I can tell you how to do it, but I have no more stock remaining."

Lizzy swallowed the lump in her throat, realizing Mrs. Robinson had practically confessed, but she wanted to be completely certain. For a moment, she was actually tempted to tell Mrs. Robinson not to say anything else, to flee quickly before there was enough for the constable to take her. It was a moment of mercy, and Lizzy found herself questioning whether justice or mercy had higher standing.

Inexorably, they were on the path toward Mrs. Robinson's apprehension though. Suspicion had already fallen on her, and she had undertaken actions that had ended two lives, no matter how miserable they were. She cleared her throat, trying to do away with the lump, and she said, "Do you know how I can obtain hemlock and make it?"

"It is easy enough, as long as you have time and access. My Henry had a touch of arthritis in his knee, so I was a good wife and obtained a special blend for him from the local apothecary. Of course, I never paid a visit to the man, but Henry didn't know that. He took his medicine faithfully for three or four days."

"It kills that quickly?" asked Lizzy with what she hoped sounded like surprise.

Mrs. Robinson snorted. "Or much faster, depending on the dose. I'd planned to kill him a lot quicker, but it took a while to figure out how the dosing worked. I could find the information on how to make it and how to identify it, but I was not so successful with how to dose it. It took a little bit of trial and error, but he was gone in less than a week. That solved my problem, and I promptly left the area before anyone could connect his death to me."

"I admire your determination to act." She wasn't being entirely insincere. In a strange way, she did admire that the woman had been brave enough to take matters into her own hands and reassert control of her future, but Lizzy could never approve of how she had done it. "And what of Lady Longe? Did you have some hemlock left?"

Mrs. Robinson nodded. "I did. It seemed like a prudent idea to bring what I had with me, and the tools to make more, should I ever need it. I could not accept what she had done to Thomas, and what she was about to do to me. Then she was going to disown poor Miss de Guille, who has never been anything but kindness itself to me and to that sweet little maid Victoria, who I suspect was never much of a maid before.

"I could not allow it to stand. I cannot allow the injustice you are facing to stand either, so come with me, girl, and I shall give you what you need to solve your problem, though you have to be prepared to move quickly after he is dispatched. You can see how easy it is to determine hemlock poisoning if you have a competent surgeon, so if they make that connection, suspicion will fall on you as his wife. Are you prepared to walk away from the life you have and live as someone else entirely?"

"No, I could never do that," said Lizzy in a gentle voice. She felt a strong hint of regret when she said, "I have not been entirely honest with you, Mrs. Robinson. Fitzwilliam did not strike me, and he would never lay a hand upon me. I have manipulated the situation so I could hear your confession in your own words."

Mrs. Robinson froze, and she looked furious for a moment. Then she surged to her feet, but she appeared to be planning to run rather than attack. She made it a few steps before Mr. Johnson stepped out from behind an arbor, and Fitzwilliam appeared from behind a collection of statues where he had taken refuge.

It took her only a moment to realize there was no escape, and her shoulders collapsed forward. She straightened them when she turned to look at Lizzy. "I suppose I always knew this day would come, but I cannot regret anything I did. I protected others and myself. You might call me a murderer, but all I did was remove two people from the world who never should have been in it to start with. I increased the happiness of everyone involved, save for those two, and I shall proudly meet my fate knowing the world is better at my hand. Shame on you for using my pain against me, Mrs. Darcy."

Lizzy flinched, bending her head. She couldn't deny she felt remorse at having done so. When she'd had the plan to appear to be an abused wife, assuming that was why Mrs. Robinson might have done away with her husband, she hadn't expected to feel any real sympathy for the woman. She hadn't considered how she would feel at twisting the situation to suit her purposes, or what pain it would dredge up for their murderess.

She looked up when a hand settled on her shoulder, recognizing Fitzwilliam's presence by his scent and his touch. He folded her into his arms, and she looked away as Mr. Johnson clapped irons around Mrs. Robinson hands and led her from the garden.

She snuggled closer to her husband, appreciating his warmth and strength. "I know I did the right thing in getting her to confess to her crimes, so why do I feel so miserable?"

Fitzwilliam put his hands around her face, gently stroking her cheeks. "You are a human with compassion and empathy. It is obvious that Mrs. Robinson has endured a great tragedy. Unfortunately, she chose to compound it. Perhaps she might have even found some forgiveness and understanding for poisoning her husband, since one could argue it was an act of self-defense, but she had no need to kill Lady Longe. That was a matter of revenge, and for that, she shall surely hang."

Lizzy nodded, understanding that. "I still feel miserable about the whole thing. Common sense suggests that solving the crime and ensuring justice makes one feel wholly positive, so why am I wretched in my success?"

He shrugged as he put his arm around her waist, drawing her against his side as they started walking slowly. "People are never straightforward, and there are levels of complexity. I suspect it is quite normal to feel ambivalent in such a situation. Will you let it deter you from future investigations, should the opportunity arise?"

Lizzy laid her head on his shoulder. "Truthfully, I do not know, Fitzwilliam. I find myself hoping to never have to make the choice again. I am content with a life of mundanity versus the highs and lows of investigating crimes. Despite my knack for it, perhaps I lack the fortitude to do it."

"Or perhaps you are the perfect person to do so, because you can see more than one side of the situation, and you can carefully weigh everything that occurs. Someone like you would do it for justice, not recognition."

She looked up at him, allowing his words to soothe some of the ache inside her. "I love you more than words can say, Fitzwilliam."

"And I love you, Lizzy. That is something that will never change."

Please sign up for Abbey's newsletter[1] to receive information about new releases. If you have any difficulties, email Abbey to request a manual add.

---

1.   https://www.subscribepage.com/JAFF

About The Author

Abbey is a diehard Jane Austen fan and has loved Fitzwilliam since the first time she "met" him at age thirteen upon borrowing the book from the school library. He is the ideal man, though Abbey's husband is a close second. Abbey enjoys writing various steamy and sweet Jane Austen variations, but "Pride & Prejudice" (and Mr. Darcy) will always be her favorite.

Did you love *Honeymoon & Hemlock*? Then you should read *Crime & Courtship: A Sweet Pride & Prejudice Mystery Romance Compilation*[1] by Abbey North!

Lizzy and Darcy meet first in Meryton and rub each other the wrong way. If not for a series of thefts requiring someone to solve the mystery, they would likely never find an accord. Working together has the unexpected effect of bringing them a new understanding, and when they thwart a kidnapping, she thinks they might have a chance at friendship and perhaps more. Then Darcy and the Netherfield party depart without word or explanation, leaving Jane (and possibly Lizzy) heartbroken. When she sees Darcy again in Hunsford, she's not sure she can forgive him even as they work together to apprehend a blackmailer. They part with animosity but are reunited in London,

---

1. https://books2read.com/u/4NyVlY

2. https://books2read.com/u/4NyVlY

finding themselves at the center of a murder investigation. When that brings them closer again, Lizzy accepts an invitation to Pemberley for Darcy to properly court her. Things seem to be going well, even with Lizzy's mother in attendance, but murder once again threatens to derail their burgeoning romance, and it also brings the return of an old Darcy nemesis.

www.ingramcontent.com/pod-product-compliance
Lightning Source LLC
Chambersburg PA
CBHW031347160726
47993CB00002B/863